Lyons fired twice, one bullet for each man

The only sounds of the killing were the slaps of the bullets punching into skulls and the actioning of the Colt's slide.

A chair scraped. Lyons turned to see three startled soldiers pushing away from a desk.

One soldier reached for a rifle and Lyons fired two quick shots into his back, slamming the dying man against the wall. Pivoting, pointing the silenced Colt with both hands, Lyons aimed at the chest of another soldier and pulled the trigger.

Nothing.

Brass stood in the slide of the Colt.

A cartridge casing had failed to eject, and the slide closed on it, jamming the action.

The odds suddenly did not look very good.

Mack Bolan's

ABLE TEAM

ABLE TEAM
Fire and
Maneuver

Dick Stivers

A GOLD EAGLE BOOK FROM
WORLDWIDE

TORONTO · NEW YORK · LONDON · PARIS
AMSTERDAM · STOCKHOLM · HAMBURG
ATHENS · MILAN · TOKYO · SYDNEY

With special thanks to
Chuck Rogers

First edition April 1985

Special thanks and acknowledgment to
G.H. Frost for his contributions to this work.

ISBN 0-373-61217-6

Printed in Canada

1

Technically, Rita Hadley violated the law.

An unemployed marine biologist with an eleven-year-old daughter, she could not afford the luxuries of movies or trips. Instead, on the days Mrs. Hadley did not get a call from a job agency—to demonstrate potato chips in a supermarket, to poll voters or type lists of addresses—she took her daughter, Shaana, to the cheap thrills of civic entertainment. Some weekends they toured the zoo or the San Diego Bay waterfront. Other times they walked through the museums. Summers and holidays offered street fairs where they could watch the tourists or shop for handcrafted gifts they could not afford.

But tonight Rita Hadley gave her daughter a front-row seat to a priceless spectacle: the sun setting into the Pacific.

Taking the public access path to the beach, then staying close to the bluffs to prevent the residents of the exclusive development above from spotting them, they walked from the public area to a quiet cove formed by a stream and the cliffs. The residents of the million-dollar homes overlooking the cove often called their security patrol to eject trespassers. But no one saw Mrs. Hadley and Shaana and they saw no one else there, saw only the gulls in the gray spring sky and the porpoises surfing the shorebreak. Bundled in their blankets against the chill wind, they watched the sun burn into the ocean.

The sea fascinated Rita Hadley. She had hoped her university training would guarantee her a career in her chosen field, but it didn't happen. Now she wanted to share her enthusiasm with Shaana. They had watched the sunset, counting the colors on the horizon and glimmering on the Pacific. Instead of returning to the televisions and shouting and smells of their apartment complex, they slept on the beach; the only sounds they heard were the waves breaking.

Violent death woke them.

They heard the struggling men. By moonlight they saw the forms. The brilliant yellow point of a flashlight zigzagged against the darkness, spotlighting a thin young man in the khaki uniform of the San Diego Parks Department, and the glistening black body of... of what?

Mrs. Hadley first thought a sea lion had attacked the Beach Ranger. Then she realized that the young man fought with a diver in a shiny black wet suit. The diver held a long, chrome knife.

"Who are—" Shaana began, before Mrs. Hadley clamped her hand over her daughter's mouth.

Could she help the ranger? Should she call for help?

Alone on the beach they had no protection but darkness. A dune and a few knots of ice plant concealed them where they lay. But if the man with the knife heard a voice or saw movement, the two trespassers could not hope to wake the residents on the bluffs above in time.

The ranger struck the diver with the flashlight again and again. But the diver's strength overwhelmed the ranger and the chrome knife streaked into his body.

As the ranger fell, Mrs. Hadley looked for an escape. Hundreds of yards of dark, deserted beach lay between them and the public access path. In the other direction, more than two hundred yards away and across the stream, she saw a public street overlooking the beach. A streetlight illuminated a parked car. But a chain link fence and a steep trail blocked that exit. If pursued, she and her daughter could not hope to run across the beach, through the stream, then scramble up the trail to the street. Too far.

Still struggling as he died, the ranger clawed at the diver's face. His hand tore away the scuba mask and Mrs. Hadley and Shaana saw the face of the killer.

They would never forget the pock-ravaged cheeks, the drooping mustache, the deep-set dark eyes of the Latin American. Grimacing with homicidal fury, the Latino drove the blade into the ranger's throat, levering the knife back and forth to sever the arteries and windpipe. Blood sprayed from the yawning wound and the Latino wrenched the knife again, the long blade severing the spinal cord and the nerves to the ranger's brain.

Already dead, the ranger spasmed as the adrenaline of his fear and panic flexed his muscles in a last, futile gesture of defense. Then he lay still, blood draining from his wounds.

Wet neoprene squeaked. The scene of death returned to darkness for a moment as the diver picked up the flashlight. Mrs. Hadley pushed her daughter flat as the murderer shone the light around, searching for possible witnesses.

Silence. The flashlight went out. Not daring to look, Mrs. Hadley kept her head down, her arm across her trembling daughter. They waited and listened, hearing neoprene squeaking and metal clanking. He must be taking off his scuba suit, Mrs. Hadley thought.

Then they heard an odd scraping noise. From time to time the murderer grunted with effort, sometimes muttering in Spanish.

Mrs. Hadley raised her head. In the darkness she saw only a black form crouching over what must have been the body of the ranger. The murderer grunted with a final effort. She heard the clink of the heavy knife against its sheath.

The murderer stood, and Mrs. Hadley went flat again, forcing her panicky breathing to slow, forcing herself to be absolutely silent.

Then she heard a splash. A few seconds later she heard another. Had the murderer returned to the ocean? But the splashes were repeated randomly, not with the rhythm of someone forcing his way through the shorebreak. Then she heard the sound of footsteps creaking through the packed sand as the murderer walked away. Metal clanked on metal as he left the beach. A minute later she heard him splash through the creek bed dividing the public beach from the private cove.

Looking up, she saw the man struggle up the steep

embankment to the street. The streetlight silhouetted him as he folded back a section of chain link. She saw his gaunt face and his heavily muscled bare shoulders as he went to the parked car and stowed the scuba equipment. A moment later he got in and started the engine—it sounded like a sports car. She saw the car as it pulled away—a Karman Ghia? The car sped toward the highway.

They waited until the engine noise faded away, then Mrs. Hadley clicked on her flashlight. She hoped she would see nothing; she hoped the fight and killing had only been a dream.

The light revealed the naked corpse of the ranger.

He was headless. Without hands, without feet.

Blood oozed from the stumps of his neck, arms and legs to flow into a vast black pool.

Rita Hadley fell to the sand and vomited.

2

Mike Chandler prepared for war.

As a prosecutor, he would fight the war with the law.

His office, in a back corner of the Organized Crime Unit of the San Diego district attorney's department, looked like a legal library this morning. Stacks of law books stood on his desk and the floor, slips of paper torn from yellow legal pads marking significant cases or key passages of juristic wisdom.

In thirty minutes he would represent the People against a murderer. A team of prominent, and expensive, criminal defense attorneys had already filed sixteen different motions for dismissal.

Leaning back in his swivel chair, glancing at the stacks of law books, Chandler nodded to himself in professional satisfaction.

"No doubt about it, Enrique Raul Castro. I'm going to put you away."

Despite his youth—he had turned thirty-five only the month before—Mike Chandler had earned the reputation as the toughest prosecutor in the district attorney's office. Six feet two inches tall, a hard-bodied one hundred eighty pounds, Chandler had fought in Golden Gloves bouts and taken trophies. A coach had once described his long arms and fists as "bullwhips to the other guy's chin." His own jaw jutted out, angular and hard-set. His brown eyes had the intense, fixed gaze of a predator.

As a prosecutor, he enjoyed the toughest, most convoluted cases, the "Chinese fire drill" crimes. Chandler appreciated the intellectual challenge.

He had served his apprenticeship in the district attorney's office prosecuting "NHI" cases, such as the beach or barroom brawls between rival motorcycle gangs that left three or four dead, where nobody knew for sure who started what or why, cases where even the friends of the deceased did not want to cooperate with the prosecution.

They said, "I'll take care of it myself."

In these cases, every potential witness, or suspect, told the police he happened to be somewhere else when the killings occurred.

For one multiple homicide case, Chandler had measured a men's room and found it to be eight feet by ten feet, with one urinal and one toilet. Thirty-five potential witnesses, or suspects, claimed to have used the men's room simultaneously.

Cynical police and the district attorney called these incidents NHI cases, meaning "no humans involved." The police processed the paperwork, going through the motions with a weary acceptance of the inevitable. Most prosecutors tried to deal the cases out, offering plea bargains of involuntary manslaughter to move the suspects through the courts and into the probation department.

Chandler had prosecuted killings as premeditated

murder. He took the cases, untangled the lies and organized the facts and evidence for a jury. He went to trial the way he had gone into the ring.

And he won.

For the past three years he had worked with the elite Organized Crime Unit. The OCU tracked the operations of sophisticated criminals and transnational drug syndicates through a shadow hell crawling with murderers, corrupt politicians, spies and informants.

The operations started with amapola poppies or coca bushes. The sticky white opium sap became the crystalline white powder of heroin. Coca leaves became coca paste, then cocaine.

Transnational syndicates made billions of dollars in pharmaceutical agriculture. They owned and operated shipping lines, truck companies, airlines. Front businesses concealed refining centers in plantations or warehouses or legitimate factories.

The syndicates employed violence, frequent and extreme, as an operational device. Routine business decisions ended competitors' careers with death, frequently in simple one-bullet hits, occasionally in military-style assaults and sometimes in hours-long ordeals of torture and mutilation preceding death.

When violence failed, the syndicates turned to their legal staffs. Renowned and respected American legal firms enjoyed unending retainers.

House counsel for organized shit, Chandler called the firms. He regarded the lawyers as partners in their clients' crimes, their exorbitant fees nothing less than profit-sharing from the blood money of drugs. Once, during a recess in a case, the defense attorney had bragged he earned eighteen hundred dollars a day while in trial.

The lawyer hired by the gangsters made more money in two days than Chandler earned in a month.

But Chandler won the case.

Now Chandler took the last minutes before the hearing to study a chart diagraming the organization of a major cocaine syndicate known as Route Five.

Made in secrecy, lubricated with blood, fueled with millions of illicit dollars, the Route Five machine transported hundreds of kilograms of cocaine a year north to the United States. Route Five began in the Bolivian Andes, moved through laboratories in Colombia, through transshipment points in Central America, to arrive in California. Coca leaves became coca paste, then cocaine, then high times at Beverly Hills parties.

Chandler knew how the drug syndicates operated. In an adjoining office, ranks of file cabinets held thousands of pages of reports and studies and case records on the workings of organized criminal enterprises—OCEs, in the jargon of prosecution.

Charts and maps covered the bland, government-beige walls of the file room. On the charts, Chandler and the other deputy district attorneys in the OCU had hand-lettered the names of syndicate commanders in red to indicate their status—Class One violators. The names of gang officers followed in columns of black. Then lines—solid blue to indicate proven links, blue dashes for suspected but unverified—connected the columns of names to various syndicates and gangs to illustrate the command structure and organization of the interlocking operations of the criminal enterprises. After each name, in parentheses, came the initials of countries indicating the primary residence or base of operations of the officer, gang, or drug source.

But the criminal enterprises did not recognize national boundaries. The transnational gangs shipped drugs from the Middle East and South America through Central America and the Caribbean to Europe and North America. Couriers carried suitcases of cash from the Northern Hemisphere to banks in Panama and Colombia for division among the subgangs and producers, then a percentage of the profit returned via electronic transfer to Miami, New York, London and Geneva.

On maps of the Americas, Chandler had used pins to illustrate the international operations of the syndicates. Black, yellow and red pins, interconnected with crisscrossing thread, created organizational schematics of narcotics production, refining, transportation and distribution.

Chandler had assembled the files, drawn the charts and stuck pins in the maps during his three years of combating the international drug conspiracies. He worked with the United States Drug Enforcement Agency, appeared in courts with allied state and federal prosecutors and assisted foreign law-enforcement agencies in their investigations and deportations of suspects.

As a continuing assignment, Chandler had studied the operations of Route Five, gathering isolated bits of information to draw the diagram of the syndicate. His aggressive style in court and his total commitment to law enforcement had gained the respect of federal and state investigators. They recognized Chandler as a qualified ally, giving him access to their files of classified and sensitive information on the operation of Route Five. Today, he would use that information.

In the years of frustrating and inconclusive work, Chandler had become the most knowledgeable source on the Route Five syndicate. District attorneys in other cities coordinated their investigations with his cases. Federal officers called him with questions. Yet on the Route Five chart, the places for the names of the upper-echelon bosses remained blank.

Chandler had a few names of suspected leaders, but nothing conclusive. The unknown gang leaders had to exist. Couriers and gunmen did not run Route Five. Like all the other syndicates, Route Five required leadership.

Enrique Raul Castro worked for Route Five. But in what capacity? A courier? An enforcer? A captain? Castro had refused to answer any questions. The Federal Bureau of Investigation files had nothing on Enrique Raul Castro, no fingerprints, no gang associations, no other names. But Chandler knew Castro had a connection to Route Five, and he would follow that connection to the leaders.

So far Castro had refused to cooperate. But would he remain silent after his conviction for murder? Cooperation could mean the difference between life in prison or execution.

Chandler had a great case. He knew it. The defense knew it. The barrage of motions filed by the defense attorneys did not dispute the facts:

A Parks and Recreation Department ranger had reported a scuba diver in trouble and had gone to give assistance.

A young woman and her daughter trespassing on a private beach had watched the scuba diver murder the ranger.

The woman had found the park ranger's walkie-talkie and put out a hysterical message that described the car the murderer drove from the beach.

An alert patrol officer on the coast highway, a rookie named Pat Murray only seven months out of the academy and one month on his own without a field training officer, had spotted the car and stopped it.

The officer saw what looked like blood in the creases of Castro's hands. He detained Castro.

The blood on Castro's hands matched the blood from the butchered ranger.

The blood on Castro's knife matched. The configuration of the knife blade matched the wounds.

When police technicians examined Castro's scuba gear, they found thirty kilos of ninety-seven-percent-pure cocaine in the right-hand tank.

In the lineup at jail, the woman and her daughter identified Castro.

Then came the final detail. At the time of his booking, Castro made a call to one of the few names on the Route Five chart, a supposedly legitimate Washington, D.C., attorney specializing in international corporate accounting. Chandler could not present the call as evidence, but the call linked Castro to Route Five.

"Deputy District Attorney Chandler?"

Chandler looked up to see Pat Murray, the alert

rookie patrol officer who had stopped Castro. "Nobody here like that," Chandler said as he stood up and extended his hand. "I'm Mike to you. Sit down. We'll be leaving for court in a couple of minutes."

"How does it look?"

"The case? Fine. There shouldn't be any problems. It's a classic case, in fact. Broadcast of crime and suspect description. Officer sees the car matching the description. Time and location fit. Blood type matching. The cocaine. Hell, it's right out of the books."

"How long is the trial going to take?"

"First we counter the motions. That'll take all day. Then the defense will horse around seeking another continuance, which I think will be denied—they've already had three postponements. We'll pick a jury. That'll take another day, minimum. Then we present the evidence. Our case will be done in two or three days, maximum. Then comes the defense, but they don't have anything. We should have a verdict in a week or two."

"What do you think he'll get?"

"Guaranteed twenty-six years to life on the 187. There's no discretion on that. The judge literally can't give him less."

"Why twenty-six? That's an odd number. Why not twenty-five or thirty?"

Chandler laughed. "Don't try to make sense of the law! Hell, all these motions we're going through don't make any sense except to give the crook a break. Who in his right mind can see the sense in kicking out key evidence, or maybe even the whole case, just because some ivory-tower idiot judge doesn't like the way you got it? But in answer to your question, the penalty is death or twenty-five to life for murder, plus an additional year for using a knife in the commission of the crime. Like a cookbook, you know?''

"What about the dope?"

"If we're lucky, he'll get five more for that. It's a 'victimless crime,' remember?''

The young officer shook his head. "Tell that to the dead lifeguard."

Chandler packed his notes and books. Already he plotted the tactics for after the conviction. Even if Castro did not get a death sentence, he faced life for murder. Chandler would offer Castro a deal that gave him federal witness protection and a reduction of prison time if Castro named the leaders of Route Five.

Castro would take the offer. The syndicate leaders would not allow a potential informer to survive long in prison. Castro knew he would be a dead man from the moment of his sentencing.

In one sense the idea of giving an animal like Castro even one day off his prison time sickened Chandler. But logic and experience told him that he had no other way of following the connection to the gang leaders.

Snapping shut his briefcase, Chandler looked at Officer Murray. "All right. Let's put away Enrique Raul Castro!"

3

Superior Court 43. Judge A. Donald Mayer, formerly a defense attorney and a past president of the California chapter of the American Civil Liberties Union, considered the first motion to suppress evidence. Under California Penal Code 1538.5, illegally gained evidence could not be presented in court.

"The actions of the arresting officer in this case represent outrageous and gestapolike attacks against the rights of my client," Matthew Ponzi, the defense attorney declared. "I respectfully petition the court to—"

"Your Honor!" Chandler interrupted. "Beginning with *Terry versus Ohio*, case after case has upheld the right of the police to stop a car that matches the description of one involved in a crime. That's what Patrolman Murray did here. There was no violation of the Fourth Amendment in that."

"But Your Honor," objected Ponzi. "Mrs. Hadley said it was a tan Volkswagen. My client was driving a Porsche, and it wasn't tan. It was brown. The officer had no right to stop him."

"Wait a minute!" Chandler lost patience with the defender. "She called it 'a tan Volkswagen, a little sports car, like a Karman Ghia.' Which is shaped much like a Porsche 912 to the untrained eye. The difference between tan and light brown is just a matter of opinion. Probably no one in this courtroom could agree on shades of color. Besides, at two in the morning there aren't many cars on the road, and here comes one that is almost identical to the description broadcast over the radio.

"And the initial detention," Chandler continued, "was simply for purposes of investigation. The officer doesn't have to be absolutely sure, or even have probable cause. All that is necessary under *Terry* and in California under *In re: Tony C.* is a reasonable suspicion the person he detains may be involved in criminal activity."

Judge Mayer looked at Ponzi. "Well, Counsel. What is your position?"

"My client wasn't breaking any law when Patrolman Murray pulled him over. The patrolman therefore violated my client's rights."

Chandler turned and gave the defense attorney a sarcastic grin. "I don't suppose learned counsel would care to share any case citations in support of his supposition."

"He doesn't have to," Judge Mayer stated. "It's a question of reasonable cause. I am inclined to believe the defendant's rights were in fact violated." The judge paused. He cocked his head to one side and stared into space. Finally, striking a pose of judicial dignity, he looked over the tops of his glasses to address the prosecutor. "The police have long oppressed the citizens, especially the poor and underprivileged. It is my duty to see the big picture, to stop that kind of conduct. It is true that under the cases cited by the prosecutor, if Mrs., uh . . . Hadley had simply called it a 'little tan car' or even simply a 'little car,' the officer would have been justified in making the stop.

"But she didn't. She called it a tan Volkswagen. In fact, it was a Porsche. And a brown one at that. That's a discrepancy I cannot overlook in my duty to rule on the propriety of the police conduct. I rule that the officer violated the defendant's rights when he stopped the Porsche Mr. Castro was driving that night."

Ponzi leaped to his feet and pressed his advantage. "Your Honor's ruling is, of course, correct. But in addition, since the stop of the car was illegal, then all the evidence that was derived because of that stop must be suppressed."

Judge Mayer turned to Chandler. "Well?"

Stunned, the prosecutor searched for words. The exclusionary rule held that any evidence obtained by an unconstitutional search could not be admitted at trial. But the search here had been clearly proper.

"Well, Counsel?" the judge repeated.

"Your Honor!" Chandler rose to his feet, his mind racing to prevent the rape of justice he feared. "The Constitution was never meant to turn criminals like this free. It only says there can't be any unreasonable searches and seizures. It's a perversion of the whole system of justice to take a criminal who's so obviously guilty and—"

"Counsel! That will be enough of that talk! I'll remind you that Mr. Castro is innocent until proved guilty. Now, if you have a legal argument make it. Or sit down."

"Legal argument? Here's your legal argument! A ranger thought he saw a diver in trouble, and Castro brutally butchered him. There were two eyewitnesses. They told the police what the escape car looked like. A good cop stopped a car that matched that description and caught the killer literally red handed, with the dead man's blood on his hands. There is nothing, I repeat, nothing, unconstitutional about that!"

The judge smiled. "Your erroneous opinions are precisely why we have judges and defense attorneys like Mr. Ponzi. You would ignore the Constitution of the United States in your rush to condemn the innocent. Unless we stop you. My ruling stands. You will offer no evidence to the jury that Mr. Castro was detained in the area, that he had the blood of the deceased on his person, that he had the murder weapon, or that he had thirty kilos of cocaine in the vehicle. Now, are you ready to proceed with the presentation of your other evidence?"

Even as the judge spoke, Chandler replotted his case. He still had two eyewitnesses. Or one adult and a minor, to be exact. Though the beach had been dark, they had identified Castro in a police lineup. He had tried and won cases with even less as evidence.

"I call Mrs. Rita Hadley to the witness stand...."

After the oath, Chandler asked Mrs. Hadley one question. "Is the man you saw murder the ranger in this court?"

"That's him." She pointed at Castro.

Then her eleven-year-old daughter took the witness chair. "I want you to be very careful, Shaana. I want you to look around the courtroom and tell us if you see the man who killed the ranger on the beach that night.''

''That's him.'' She pointed at Enrique Raul Castro.

''Are you sure?''

''Yes, sir.'' She nodded her head, her eyes wide and solemn. ''I'll never forget his face.''

Chandler turned to Judge Mayer. ''Your Honor, the prosecution is ready to begin jury selection.''

THE NEXT MORNING Chandler went to Hank's Gym to prepare for his day in court. The dingy downtown building had a gym that featured a dirty cement floor, a wall of cracked mirrors and thousands of pounds of weights. No exercise bicycles, no carpets, no aerobic classes, no co-ed Jacuzzis, no women.

In a second room, boxers worked out on speed bags and heavy bags, or sparred with one another in a practice ring.

Chandler had been born and raised in a conservative, upper-middle-class ivy-league home. His parents had had great expectations for his future. The university, an executive position with a major corporation, perhaps a second career in diplomacy or politics. Chandler spent most of his youth rebelling. When his friends started tennis lessons, Chandler found a slum gym and learned to fight. When his college friends joined fraternities, Chandler joined ROTC. His friends went on to graduate school for masters degrees in business administration. Chandler went to a fire base in II Corps, Vietnam.

To begin his workout, Chandler did push-ups, pull-ups and abdominal crunches. He rushed through an intense session with the weights before going to the heavy bag. He attacked the hundred pounds of leather and rags with savage fury, imagining that his fists pulped and broke Enrique Raul Castro's body.

When he finished, sweat dripped from his body to the hardwood floor—unlike the gym, the boxing room had the luxury of hardwood floors. Chandler went to the lockers with his fists and arms aching, but his mind clear. As he stripped, his body flowing with sweat, he told himself again and again, "I'm going to get him, and I'm going to get his gang."

MOMENTS AFTER JUDGE MAYER called the crowded courtroom to order, Counselor Ponzi leaped to his feet. "Your Honor, before we begin voir dire, I wish to know if Mr. Chandler really intends to go forward with this case. Now that the court has ruled ninety percent of his evidence was seized illegally, I want to make sure this isn't just some delay to harass my client."

"Well, Counsel?" Judge Mayer asked.

Chandler stood to counter the motion, saying, "Ready for the People."

"But Your Honor, this is just a waste of time in view of yesterday's ruling. Mr. Chandler should concede the police acted improperly and abandon the case. And if he won't, perhaps Your Honor should dismiss the charges. For Mr. Chandler to pursue this case, given the present state of the evidence, is a clear denial of due process and is obviously only vindictive prosecution."

"What is your response, Mr. Chandler? Do you have enough evidence to proceed?"

"The police didn't act improperly at all! It's the law that's improper. But we're stuck with it, and that's that. Yes, I do have sufficient evidence to proceed. I suggest that counsel recall that under California law the uncorroborated testimony of a single witness, whom the jury believes, is legally sufficient for a conviction. Perhaps counsel is forgetting I have two eyewitnesses, more than enough to send—"

"Do you?" Ponzi asked.

Chandler looked to the defense table. Ponzi sat expressionless, staring into space. But Castro grinned at Chandler. A vague, formless dread formed in Chandler's mind. At that moment, he saw Detective Chuck Jenner of Homicide ease through the courtroom doors and hurry forward. The detective motioned to him.

Leaning over the railing dividing the spectators from the court officers, Jenner whispered, "They found Mrs. Rita Hadley and Shaana Hadley shot about an hour ago. Bullets through the head, execution style. Your subpoena was stuck in Mrs. Hadley's mouth."

Staggering backward, Chandler fell against the prosecution table. He found himself strangely detached from the proceedings, as if he looked down on the courtroom from a point in space.

How many must die, he thought.

If the judge hadn't thrown out all the other evidence, leaving only the testimony of the woman and girl, they wouldn't have been killed.

Chandler looked around him. The detective stood at the rail. The spectators watched him. Ponzi gathered his notes and closed his briefcase. Enrique Raul Castro laughed.

Lurching upright, a fist cocking back, Chandler stepped toward Castro. But the detective vaulted the rail and caught him. "Stop, Mike, they'll put you away! Stop!"

In the background, Judge Mayer hammered the gavel down. "Order! Order!"

Weaving on his feet, as if a punch had knocked him unconscious but he had not fallen, Chandler turned to the judge. He pulled down a deep breath and announced, "Your Honor, I have been informed by Detective Jenner that police discovered my witnesses murdered. I will not be able to proceed with the prosecution. The People rest."

He slumped down in his chair and stared at his hands, oblivious of the voices around him. Spectators and reporters questioned him. He did not answer. The reporters shouted questions to Detective Jenner. Then the bailiffs herded the crowd out of the courtroom.

"Tough case, Mike. Went bad for you from the start."

Chandler looked up to see Ponzi extending a hand. For a handshake. He stared at the pale, uncallused hand until Ponzi pulled it back.

Ponzi shrugged. "Take it easy. Lighten up on yourself. You did your job, I did mine. I gotta go through the motions to earn my fee and keep the client happy, you understand?"

"Just like the whore you are," Chandler told him. "Except that prostitutes don't claim they're upholding the Constitution."

Clenching his fist for an instant, Ponzi stared at the prosecutor. But he hurried away without another word. In the silence of the empty courtroom, Chandler assembled his books and papers.

When he turned, he saw the blond-haired man who waited in the back-row spectator seats. A wide-shouldered man with a face made leathery by exposure to the weather, he wore a sports coat and slacks. He stood, removing his sunglasses, as Chandler approached.

Ice-blue eyes fixed on the prosecutor as the man extended his hand. "Mr. Chandler, I'd like to talk to you about Enrique Raul Castro and the Route Five syndicate."

Still dazed, Chandler shook the man's hand. He felt strength and tendons like steel in the grip. "Why?" he asked.

The man glanced behind him. Alone in the spectator section, they could not be overheard.

"Because Castro and all his gang deserve to die."

4

"Who are you?" Chandler demanded.

Carl Lyons slipped on his sunglasses. "My friends call me Ironman. You have any other cases scheduled this morning, Mr. Chandler?"

"You still haven't told me who you are. You a cop?"

"I used to be."

"Here in San Diego? I don't know you."

"LAPD."

"That still doesn't tell me what you are now and why you want to talk to me."

Chandler saw himself in the mirrors of the stranger's sunglasses. For a second the man looked at Chandler, studying him—his expressions, the pulse at his throat, the angle of his shoulders, his grip on the briefcase. Then the mirror-eyed mask broke. Smiling, Lyons told him, "I'm federal now. Special assignment for the Justice Department. And the assignment is Enrique Raul Castro."

"Then your assignment's canceled because that psycho is walking out the door as soon as 'Set Them Free Mayer' sends the papers over to the jail. Bastard sees his life's work as turning killers loose on the public."

"I know."

"Of course, what the hell does he care? He lives in a big fancy house in La Jolla. Only crime he ever sees, apart from his kids dealing dope with their rich-kid buddies, is if his car gets smashed by a drunk or his house gets ripped off. And then it's nothing but padding insurance claims so he ends up making money. You got some credentials to go with your special assignment?"

Lyons smiled and shook his head.

Stepping past the stranger, the prosecutor told him, "You want to talk to me? Come back with some identification that tells me who you are and what your special assignment is, understand?"

"Want identification? How about...Whiskey Dog?"

Chandler stopped at the doors. "What did you say?"

"You heard me."

"Yeah, I did. But there's more, isn't there? There's a name."

"Bolan."

"And the first name? And rank?"

"Sergeant Mack Bolan."

"He send you?"

"Like I said, I'm federal now. The department sent me. But I checked you out with Mack."

"I heard he was dead."

"Bolan dead?" Carl Lyons laughed. "He's too young to die, and there's no one who can kill him, so how's Mack going to get dead?"

Chandler motioned Lyons through the courtroom door. "You want to talk? Where?"

THEY WALKED FROM THE COURTHOUSE to La Cantina, a long narrow café between a shoe store and a television-repair shop. Chandler ate there when he wanted to avoid his courthouse associates or to talk with police between their shifts. The patrons had to speak Spanish. The Mexican waitresses and non-English menus kept the tourists away. At the café, Chandler met the partners of the stranger who called himself the Ironman.

Lyons had introduced Gadgets Schwarz as the team electronics specialist. He looked more like a professor and athlete than a technician, his body hard, his face tanned, his dark hair shot with the sun-bleached streaks of an outdoorsman.

The other man, Rosario Blancanales, the Politician, had the same hard physique. Premature gray streaked his hair. He flashed smiles to the waitress and café owner as though they had been his friends for years. Though Chandler spoke only basic Spanish, he heard the Politician speak to the waitress in Mexican patois, dropping his pronouns and using half-English, half-Spanish jargon to question her about the menu. But when he discussed the newspaper headlines with the café owner, the Politician switched to Castilian, using the formal tense and a university vocabulary to praise the owner's intuitive understanding of the social issues unmentioned in the front page stories.

"In a way," Lyons commented, "it's to our advantage that you lost the case."

"Glad it's to someone's advantage. But it didn't do much for justice. Castro and his gang murdered three good people and he laughed about it."

"Don't sweat it," Gadgets reassured him. "El Rique will get his, approximately."

"What do you mean, 'approximately'?"

Gadgets grinned. "One problem with justice is that you can only cross out scum once."

The Ironman laughed. "But the Wizard's working on a machine for endless instant replays."

"Yeah, an endless loop of payback. Just for El Rique."

The Politician interrupted the jokes. "Where do you know Mack from?"

"Long time ago," Chandler said. "I was a new second lieutenant who didn't know shit about anything. Thought I was a tough guy in the university because I could punch it out in a boxing ring. And then I'm in the highlands and we're punching it point-blank with automatic rifles. Did I learn quick. You take it on the chin with an RPG, you don't ask your manager for a rematch. The sergeant did me a favor. He taught me to think in ways that helped me stay alive and keep my platoon alive. Told me to stop thinking like a university-educated second lieutenant and put myself in the place of the enemy. That kept me alive—and my men alive—when a lot of other officers went by the book and went home by the box."

"Yeah," Gadgets agreed. "Think like the enemy. That's one thing we do all the time. You see me there?"

"You?" Chandler searched his memory, faces flashing through his mind. "No, I don't."

"Flower Child?"

"Yeah! The guy with the peace symbol. Him, I remember. Said he was a pacifist. 'Someone give you trouble, pacify them.' Where's he now?''

"Gone."

"What do you mean?"

"Gone where dead men go. What about this Whiskey Dog jive? When did the sarge tell you that?''

"We were putting down a bottle of Jack Daniel's. Laughing and talking about lieutenants. And we're at the bottom of the bottle and he looks at it and says 'Whiskey Dog.' I thought it was a landing zone. I asked him what happened there. He stares off into space and says it again, 'Whiskey Dog,' and downs the last of the bottle.''

Lyons looked at his partners. "Bolan drinking?"

"He used to be a fun guy," Gadgets commented. "When he came home, he got serious. So what does it mean?"

"You tell me."

"He said it was a code phrase you'd recognize," the Ironman said. "He said you'd know all about it.''

"I thought it meant 'weaklings die.' But after a year in the field, I thought it meant, 'warriors die.' Never did work it out. And Bolan never came back to my fire base. But back to business. What's your interest in Castro?''

"We want the leaders of Route Five," the Ironman answered.

"So do I. I've worked on that syndicate for years."

"That's why we want you to go with us."

"Where?"

"When Castro gets out—" Lyons glanced at his watch "—we'll follow him. Where he goes, we go."

Chandler shook his head. "Maybe you have authorization for international investigation, but I don't. I can't follow him out of California. I can't help you unless you bring him back here.''

Gadgets laughed. Lyons looked at his partners and said, ''Mr. Chandler doesn't understand. Counselor, we'll bring back information. Maybe a prisoner. But the gang, all of them. . . .'' Ironman dismissed the idea with a backhand gesture.

''What do you mean? If you don't bring them back to the United States, there's no chance for prosecution.''

''One question,'' Gadgets asked. ''When you popped the Cong, did you read them their rights and schedule a court appearance?''

''No way!'' Chandler laughed. ''They were the enemy. It was war. It was kill or be killed.''

''So understand,'' Lyons continued. ''We're asking you straight out. Route Five is the enemy. Do you want to go to war?''

Chandler almost laughed. The three men watched him, their eyes on him, waiting for his answer. Only a few hours ago, he had beaten his fists against the gym's heavy bag, imagining that he beat Castro and Ponzi and all of the gangsters responsible for the murder of the ranger on the beach that night. And that had been before he learned of the executions of the young woman and her daughter. Now these strangers offered him what he knew he wanted: the opportunity to fight the syndicate on its own terms. No law. No quarter. No limits but firepower and death.

His mouth had gone dry. Not daring to answer and risk his voice cracking, he nodded.

War.

ENRIQUE RAUL CASTRO walked out of the San Diego county jail that afternoon. From a van on the street Chandler watched Castro drive his Porsche from the impound lot. Lyons started the van's engine and turned into traffic. Beside Chandler, Gadgets monitored the directional finder and minimicrophone transmitters he had placed in the Porsche earlier that day.

"We're on our way," Chandler commented.

"And where we stop," Gadgets added as he keyed his hand radio, "nobody knows. Political? How's your receiver working?"

Blancanales followed the van in a nondescript rented sedan. "Steady beep. But only road noise from the audio."

"He's stopping!" Lyons reported from the front. "Tell Pol to keep him in sight. We'll go past and circle."

As Gadgets passed the instructions to his partner in the rented car, Chandler looked through the van's tinted side window to see the Porsche pull up to a telephone box at the corner of a service station lot. Then they continued past and he lost sight of the murderer.

Pol's voice came from the hand radio. "He's making a call."

"Keep him in sight," Gadgets said as the van made a right turn. "We're starting around."

After the call, Castro continued to the freeway and went south at a modest sixty miles an hour. The van and the rented sedan paced the Porsche. Staying close in the metropolitan traffic, Lyons drove smoothly, easing from lane to lane, keeping the German sports car in sight. Blancanales stayed several car lengths back, watching the van instead of the Porsche. As the traffic thinned, he let the sedan slow until he trailed a half minute behind his partners.

"He'll cross the border," Chandler said. "Think we can stay with him through Tiajuana?"

Gadgets pointed to the UHF receiver. "With this gear, we can follow him anywhere."

But when the freeway ended at the international border, Castro did not continue into the Tiajuana lanes. Instead he parked the Porsche in a public lot. Lyons steered into the lines of cars and trucks bound for Mexico as Gadgets radioed their partner. "He's crossing over on foot...and he's taking a taxi."

"Stay with him," Pol responded.

Looking through the back window, Chandler saw the cabdriver swerve through the southbound traffic. Chandler called forward to Lyons. "Turn! He's going to the airport."

"Take the airport lane, Pol!" Gadgets relayed.

Brakes shrieked, the van lurched. Cursing under his breath, Lyons waited for a truck to speed past, then he swerved and accelerated. The taxi carrying Castro flashed past the van, the muffler of the battered yellow Dodge roaring. Lyons kept the taxi in sight. A few minutes later, the taxi stopped in front of the airport's terminal.

Lyons passed the terminal and parked the van where they could watch all the doors. Seconds later, Blancanales parked the rented sedan.

"Going in. My Beretta's under the seat. The keys are in the ignition."

"Stay with him," Gadgets replied.

WITHOUT LOOKING BACK at the van, Blancanales hurried through the parked cars and lines of waiting taxis. Porters saw that he carried no luggage and ignored him. He pushed through the plate-glass doors of the terminal and scanned the crowds. Castro stood in a ticket line.

Blancanales stepped into the line. Waiting behind Castro, he kept his eyes on the arrival-departure board. Several flights were scheduled to leave in the next hour. One went directly to Mexico City, others hopped through the cities of the northern states before finally arriving in the capital. Blancanales waited.

When it was Castro's turn at the ticket counter, he asked for a flight which it turned out left in only ten minutes. The plane stopped in the resort city of Mazatlán for an hour, then continued on to Mexico City. Blancanales looked over the murderer's shoulder and watched him pay with a credit card.

Taking the ticket, Castro went to the departure gate. Blancanales asked for a ticket on the same flight. He kept Castro in sight as the airline clerk filled out the ticket and gave him change for his dollars. With a handful of hundred-peso notes, Blancanales left the terminal. He dodged around to the side of the exit where he could not be seen from inside the terminal, then keyed his hand radio.

"He's going to Mazatlán, then Mexico City. I've got a ticket on the same plane. I'll call Stonyman when I know where he's gone."

"We'll arrange a flight," Lyons answered. "We'll try to be there before you."

"Then hurry. See you there."

Blancanales saw Gadgets leave the van and run to the rented sedan. Both vehicles left the parking lot. Pocketing the radio, Blancanales returned to the terminal and hurried to the departure lounge. A line of passengers stood waiting at the door as a steward checked their boarding passes. Blancanales went through last.

The ramp connected to the rear door of the jetliner. As he searched for his seat, Blancanales scanned the rows of seated passengers. He did not see Castro in the few rows he passed. He found his seat but continued past.

In Spanish, a stewardess asked him to take his seat and fasten his safety belt. Blancanales pretended not to understand. "What?"

The young Mexicana switched to softly accented English. "Please be seated, sir. We are leaving immediately."

"Sure, yeah, I will." Blancanales stood aside for her to pass, then continued forward.

At the rear of the plane, the stewardess pulled the door closed. Blancanales felt the jet vibrating as the pilot gave the engines power. With a lurch, the jet taxied. Blancanales continued to the front of the passenger compartment, glancing at his ticket as if searching for his seat. He had not seen Castro.

Another stewardess told him to take his seat. Blancanales turned and went back, checking every face in the plane.

No Castro.

The engines shrieked. Acceleration threw Blancanales into his seat. Cursing under his breath, Blancanales fastened his safety belt. He slipped out his hand radio. Hiding it inside his coat, he keyed the transmit again and again.

Nothing. His partners had already gone out of transmission range.

Then the jet lifted away, taking Blancanales to Mazatlán.

5

After crossing the United States-Mexican border at the San Ysidro checkpoint, Gadgets buzzed his partner in the van. "I'm staying with the Porsche. You go ahead and make the calls, okay?"

"No problem, except...." The transmission cut off.

"Except what?" Steering with one hand, Gadgets left the freeway. He made two left turns and took a southbound onramp. On the opposite side of the freeway, he saw the van continuing to the north.

"Except we'll be out of radio range. So use the prosecutor's phone tape for messages. He's got a remote beeper to play back the calls." Lyons gave him a phone number. "Got that? You call, leave a phone number, then we can call you back."

"Hey, don't go back to San Diego. Make your calls from a phone around here. I want you as backup, in case someone shows up quick fast to pick up the Porsche."

"Oh, yeah. Will do, Wizard. Getting off now."

Flashing yellow lights warned of the end of the freeway. Gadgets slowed and eased to the right. He turned into the parking lot. Tourists returning from a day of shopping packed piñatas and clay pots in their cars.

Servicemen parked their cars for an evening in the bars of Tiajuana. Gadgets waited, the rented car idling in neutral, as a carload of hard-muscled young men with the white-sidewall haircuts of the U.S. Marines threw karate kicks at one another. One Marine stepped back to avoid a kick and fell backward over Castro's Porsche.

No alarm, Gadgets noted.

The Marines continued to the border crossing. Gadgets found a parking place where he could watch the Porsche in his rearview mirrors. Sitting low in the seat, he turned the DF minimike receiver down to an almost inaudible beeping. He watched the mirrors and waited.

"DAVIS, DEA, SPEAKING."

"Pete Davis?" Lyons was calling from a pay phone a few off ramps north of the border. Chandler waited in the van, monitoring the radio and the UHF receiver. "This is Specialist Number One. You know me from the Ochoa adventure. Want to take another flight down south?"

"The three-man carnival of surprises? Able to go anywhere, do anything—"

"This is an open line," Lyons cautioned him.

"I'm not saying any names. But I want to know if you're asking for a pilot and a plane or if you're organizing another disaster."

"Straight flight."

"Said that last time."

"No, you said that last time. Then your agency arranged for an antiaircraft ambush. This time, you won't know—and no one in your agency will know—where we're going until the plane lands.''

''I think the security problem is fixed. There were some transfers and terminations.''

''Willing to bet your life on that?'' Lyons asked the pilot.

''Well, ah....'' Davis hesitated. Finally, he laughed and said, ''Like you suggested, tell me where I'm going when we're airborne. When do you need to leave?''

''Immediately. Can you do that?''

''I'll switch a flight with another guy. Tell me, this mission is authorized, correct?''

''Most definitely.''

''You got an officer in the bureaucracy I can most definitely check with?''

Lyons gave him the Stonyman number and access code for the day. ''Get the plane ready. Fuel it for maximum flight time. We're on our way now.''

''Will do. And no matter what you say, just in case, I'm bringing my survival gear.''

Chandler called out from the van. ''Ironman! The Wizard's spotted a pickup team!''

''Got to go!'' Lyons hung up. The pay phone immediately rang as the operator called back for the overtime charges. Lyons left the phone ringing as he ran back to the van. As he started the engine, he keyed his hand radio's transmit key. ''Ironman talking.''

''Be ready to move. Some hoods just showed up....''

TWO LATINOS in shimmering rayon jackets got into the Porsche. A third young man waited in the Cadillac until he saw the Porsche leave the parking place, then both cars left for the northbound lanes of the freeway. Gadgets did not follow immediately. He keyed his hand radio and said, "They're on their way. Three of them came in a Cadillac Seville, dark blue, white sidewalls, wire wheels. Couldn't get the license number. One Chicano's driving the Cadillac. Two are in the Porsche. I'm leaving now. The two cars are probably two minutes from you."

"Hitting the freeway," Lyons told him. "We'll hold it down to fifty per hour until they come up behind us."

"The pilot say we'll have a plane?"

"We got it."

"Destination unknown," Gadgets said as he set down his radio. Turning up the UHF receiver, he heard a steady beeping. From the audio frequency, he heard a roar of road noise and then rock music. He could not distinguish the voices in the noise.

On the northbound freeway, he accelerated into an express lane and passed the other traffic. He saw the Cadillac ahead. Cutting across two lanes, he slipped behind a semitrailer. The trailer blocked his view of the Cadillac but also denied the Latino driver any chance of spotting the surveillance.

"This is the Wizard," Gadgets radioed. "I'm about ten car lengths behind the Caddy."

In the back of the van, Chandler watched the onrushing traffic. He pressed down the transmit key of the unfamiliar radio. "Prosecutor here. Haven't seen them yet. Any chance the Porsche could've gotten off?"

"Listen to the beep. Steady, right? If they get off, you'll know it."

Setting down the hand radio, Chandler called to Lyons. "Any chance they could be scanning your radio frequency?"

"No chance. Those radios are designed and made by the National Security Agency. Every transmission is encoded and decoded. All they'd hear is static noise if they found our frequency."

"Any chance they could decode it?"

"We've had scares. One time we ran into a gang that had the same kind of equipment. But as far as we know, we've never been intercepted."

"Where'd the gang get the scrambler equipment?"

"Same place we did. The NSA."

"They stole it?"

"No. They have people inside supplying them."

"A gang? What do you mean?"

"A neo-Nazi gang that ran drugs. A very organized operation. Very high connections in the U.S. and in other countries. Made all kinds of problems for us."

"Like what?"

"Like getting our plane shot down. Like getting ambushed. That's one of the reasons we're taking you along. You know what goes with the Route Five gang and we don't. If we request information or liaison, we're tipping off their people that we're on the way."

"You think the gangs have got people in the DEA and the Justice Department? No way! Impossible!"

The man that Chandler knew only as Ironman turned and smiled a death's-head grin. "I *know* they do," he said. "You don't, but you're going to find out."

"I don't believe it."

"The fascists and gangsters have got goons in the federal agencies. Wish it wasn't true, but it's a fact. Makes operating very—"

"The Porsche!" Chandler interrupted. "In the second lane from the divider."

"I see it." Lyons accelerated to match the speed of the sports car.

"And there's the Cadillac."

"Report it to the Wizard. Here we go. . . ."

As THE AFTERNOON became dusk, they followed the Porsche to a La Jolla condominium complex. A traffic signal delayed the Cadillac. Lyons guided the van into a parking place in the deep shadow of an overhanging tree.

Like a real-estate developer's brochure, the two sides of the street illustrated the past and the future of the exclusive suburb of San Diego. On one side of the hillside street, bungalows and duplexes from the 1940s overlooked La Jolla Cove and the horizon-spanning expanse of the Pacific. On the other side of the street, new condominiums rose to three stories to capture the same view.

The condos featured street-level garages. From the back of the van, Chandler watched one Latino open a garage door and the other drive the Porsche inside. When the engine switched off, he heard voices and movement echoing inside the garage. Chandler turned up the receiver's volume.

Gadgets's voice came from the walkie-talkie. "Hit the tape recorder!"

Listening, Chandler found the cassette recorder's button and pressed it. The voices continued for a moment. Then he heard the faint squeal of brakes and another voice.

"The Cadillac just pulled up," Lyons told him.

Chandler only nodded. He mentally noted words and phrases and the inflections of the voices. Then the voices faded and the shriek of garage door springs terminated the talk. He looked up and saw the two men getting into the Cadillac.

"Wizard, the Cadillac's moving. You take the lead. We'll come up behind."

"Moving."

Lyons turned to Chandler. "What did they say?"

"Something about El Pajaro. . . that they had to get back to the boat before the 'shit' did. A boat! Yeah, Castro brought in his cocaine from a boat."

Guiding the van through the evening traffic, Lyons nodded. "Makes sense." He keyed his hand radio. "Wizard, I think I got them in sight. Where are you?"

"One car back."

"The prosecutor says they're going to a boat called the *Bird*. You hear that?"

"More or less. But what's the 'shit' they're talking about? Think maybe we can intercept another shipment of dope?"

Chandler laughed. "Tell him to forget it. No judge I know would issue a warrant based on what we've pulled this afternoon. Unless maybe it was a warrant for my arrest—"

Gadgets's voice interrupted Chandler's speculation. "They're getting on the freeway again, going north."

Lyons called back to Chandler. "What's the closest private harbor to the north?"

NINETY MINUTES LATER, Lyons and Chandler stripped to their underwear and slipped into the frigid water by the Dana Point Marina on the coast of southern Orange County. Gadgets took their clothes and returned to where they had parked the van, only a few steps away from the water.

"Cold!" Chandler muttered.

"We'll be done in ten minutes."

Sidestroking silently, Lyons led Chandler along the concrete seawall to the total darkness under the pier walkway, then they swam quickly past the sterns of the moored craft.

Voices and music came from the yachts and cabin cruisers. On the concrete walkway, they heard footsteps, the light footsteps of a woman, then the slapping bare feet of a man. The woman protested, then a beer bottle splashed into the black water. But Lyons and Chandler left the argument behind. Dog-paddling, Chandler kept his head above the water. He smelled diesel oil and gasoline and human filth from the toilets of the boats.

They came to a stern lettered with the name *El Pajaro Blanco*. Someone paced the walkway. Other footsteps sounded on the deck of the yacht. Lyons and Chandler stayed against the slick fiberglass of the hull.

Lights from the yacht illuminated the concrete

berth. At the stern of the yacht, reflected lights from the other boats and the marina shops shimmered. But the narrow space between the hull and the concrete berth remained shadowed, leaving the hull and a band of water in total darkness. Lyons pointed to the narrow space.

Above them, on the deck of the yacht, men spoke in Spanish. Lyons and Chandler waited until the footsteps on the dock walkway went one direction, then they took two strokes into the shadows at the side of the yacht. They moved along the curve of the hull until they treaded water directly beneath the voices. The lights projected shadows onto the berth.

Lyons whispered to Chandler, "You listen, I'll do the placement."

Chandler nodded. Above them, the two men still talked. An intercom buzzed. One voice answered the phone, grunting monosyllabic answers. The phone clicked down, and the voice called out, *"¡Enrique! Su abogado esta aquí."*

His lawyer? Chandler listened. He heard the voice of Enrique Raul Castro join the conversation. The murderer who had laughed at American justice complained to the other men the mountains would be too much punishment. The men countered that he could be in a prison now. Castro continued complaining that the nearest whorehouse would be in Medellín.

Medellín! One of the mountain cities of Colombia. Known as the cocaine capital of Colombia. That meant the ranch where Castro would be exiled would be somewhere within driving distance of Medellín.

Lyons hissed to Chandler. "We've struck gold. Let's go."

They sidestroked to the stern of the yacht. Rapid footsteps approached. Flat against the hull, they listened as the guard greeted a visitor with an accented "Good night, *señor*."

The footsteps went up the gangplank. Lyons and Chandler swam away. In a few minutes, they scaled the seawall and, sprinting past a surprised couple pushing a baby carriage, ran to the van. They took turns wiping oil and filth from their skin with the towel from Chandler's gym bag.

"Is that lawyer someone named Matthew Ponzi?" Chandler asked Gadgets.

"No," the Wizard said as he signaled Chandler to wait. "He's a lawyer from Washington, D.C. They're talking about his flight. . . . No, Rique's flight to. . . ."

"I heard them mention Medellín. That's a city in Colombia. That's where he'll be going."

Gadgets nodded. He checked the cassette recorder, then took off his headphone. "The lawyer brought him the tickets. And he's going tonight. Now we know where we're going."

"Medellín," Chandler repeated, not quite believing what he would do. Only this morning, he had lost his case against Castro, and with it, his hope of cracking Route Five. But now, with these three compatriots of a sniper sergeant he had known a decade ago, he would pursue Route Five into the heart of the gang's territory, the Colombian Andes.

6

Colonel José Alvarado Castro paced the balcony of his office. From time to time he paused to look out at the green Magdalena wilderness. The jungle continued into the distance, fading to a smear of color, the pale green horizon finally merging with the pale blue of the sky. Only the rectangles of the colonel's plantations broke the green expanse. In the other direction, he was presented a view of the distant peaks of the Cordillera Central de los Andes.

The colonel owned all that he saw. He owned the plantations, the roads, the trucks, the campesinos. To the people of the vast *finca*, he represented the government. He exercised the power of life and death over his Colombian army troops, his private army and all the others he employed or owned as slaves. His military strength and wealth projected his power from this wilderness to the capital of Colombia, Bogotá. His influence continued as far north as the capital of the United States, Washington, D.C.

In Colombia, the military and civilian leaders consulted with him before announcing government policies. But beyond his country's boundaries, his direct power faded. He influenced other governments with his payments of U.S. dollars to politicians, but his wealth did not buy absolute control.

Now, he felt fear. His power had been tested by an obscure prosecutor in a small North American city. Though the wealth of Colonel Castro overwhelmed the challenge, the fear remained. The North Americans, in their self-righteous and hypocritical campaign against his international enterprise, might somehow again seize his only son and the heir to all his land and wealth and power.

That morning a shortwave message had relayed the news of the court in San Diego, California, dismissing the charges against his son Enrique. Another transmission told him of Enrique's departure on a commercial flight for Colombia. But until his son actually arrived at the garrison's airstrip, his safety and freedom remained uncertain.

True, his son had brought the trouble on himself. If Enrique had not attempted the smuggling of the thirty kilos of cocaine—an insignificant amount not justified by the few hundred thousand dollars Enrique would have gained—then there would have been no arrest, no jailing, no need for lawyers and legal maneuverings.

The colonel regretted his son's foolishness. Staring out at the mountains and valleys of the vast plantation his own father had created in the Magdalena wilderness, the colonel wondered if his son could meet the challenges of a changing world.

Spanning the horizons, *la finca* existed as a monument to the daring and ruthlessness of the colonel's father, General Alejandro Castro. Enrique's grandfather. The general had scorned all laws. He had recognized no limits but his own imagination.

To create *la finca* from the vast wilderness, the general needed workers. He sent his army against the *indigena* tribes inhabiting the region, taking thousands of slaves and eliminating resistance to his enterprise. The slaves cleared the forests and hacked out hundreds of miles of interconnecting roads, unknown numbers of workers dying over the decades— killed by disease, overseers, snakes and other *indigenas* defending their ancestral territories—before the general conquered the jungle.

Throughout the first half of the century the plantation produced bananas for North America, harvested by *indigena* and *mestizo* campesinos. The general's trucks transported the crop to the Magdalena River. Barges floated the crop down to the harbor at Barranquilla for transfer to the freighters that carried the bananas to the markets of the East Coast of the United States.

Bananas, and a few finds of gold and emeralds, made the Castro family wealthy beyond the general's dreams. His millions of American dollars bought a Castilian wife and a series of blond mistresses. Colombia's finest Creole dynasties accepted the scarred, sadistic general into their elegant society. And his private army, armed with the most modern rifles, machine guns, light artillery, and eventually aircraft, assured him of a dominating position in the group of generals ruling Colombia.

But in time, the general lost his control of the banana trade. North American companies organized their own plantations in Guatemala, El Salvador and Honduras. Their fleets of steamships shuttled between Central America and the harbors of both coasts of the United States. The general squandered his investments on continuing the pretense of unlimited wealth, maintaining his army, his European mistresses and his estates. His son inherited empty mansions and a *finca* returning to the jungle.

The general's son met and overcame the challenge. During his education and military training in the United States, José Alvarado Castro had learned the history and customs of the North Americans. He read of prohibition and realized that without illegal alcohol, the underworld syndicates would have never earned the uncountable millions of dollars required to establish the Mafia. He saw a corresponding opportunity in the illegal heroin trade. He flew to Turkey and bought a few thousand amapola poppy seeds. But the campesino workers did not understand the delicate and time-consuming procedures required to bleed the poppies of opium.

However, in the early 1960s, when the youth of America discovered the counterculture ritual of marijuana smoking, the colonel realized his isolated *finca* again had a crop to offer North America. The poor campesinos of Colombia had always smoked marijuana as a cheap alternative to expensive beer and liquor. The workers required no training in the cultivation and harvesting of the plants. Untended, unfertilized marijuana seemed to explode from the soil, rising to heights of trees. His campesinos simply hacked down the plants and pressed them into bricks.

The colonel regained his family's wealth through the creation of a syndicate that managed the flow of marijuana from soil, to harvest, to shipment, to distribution. The colonel demanded absolute loyalty and secrecy. No outsiders compromised the security of his syndicate. Only trusted campesinos worked with the crop. Only faithful employees drove the trucks owned by Castro. Only his own officers headed the paper corporations that chartered his freighters to ship his crop. Only his officers commanded the gangs who distributed the crop to the North Americans. And only his bankers and attorneys handled the transfer of funds from the United States and Europe to his banks in Colombia.

Any trusted employee—campesino, army officer, North American banker—who cheated the colonel or betrayed him to a rival syndicate or law-enforcement agency died at the hands of specially selected and trained execution units.

The Castro syndicate remained untouched by the United States antidrug campaigns throughout the sixties and seventies. Yet the wealth of Colonel Castro eventually faced a threat he could not counter with bribes or deadly discipline.

Yankee enterprise.

Recognizing the multibillion-dollar market for marijuana, North Americans finally planted their own crops. University-trained botanists in Hawaii and California produced exotic hybrids of sinsemilla marijuana—hypnotic, hallucinogenic, euphoric, erotic—superior to any offered by Colombia. Even the East Coast states, the states with bootlegger traditions, produced marijuana acceptable in quality and cheaper for the unsophisticated smokers of New York City and the Eastern Seaboard.

Cocaine had already become an important second product for the colonel. But the cocaine trade made the colonel uneasy. His plantations did not grow the coca bushes that supplied the base material for his cocaine refineries. Coca only grew high in the Andes of southern Colombia, Peru and Bolivia. Quechas, the impoverished survivors of the Spanish-devastation of indigenous Andean nations, harvested the age-old stimulant drug. Gangs of *mestizo* middlemen collected and transported the thousands of pounds of coca leaves to crude laboratories, where workers used primitive chemical procedures to reduce the leaves to coca paste. Only then did the colonel's employees enter the chain of production and marketing of the drug. His men bought the paste, and his pilots flew it to his laboratories in the cool mountains overlooking the *finca*. From the moment his men purchased the paste to the sale of the pure cocaine in the United States, the colonel maintained absolute control.

But he did not control the coca fields, the harvest, or the first steps of the refining process. At any time, the suppliers in the Andes might cut his syndicate out of the trade, leaving Colonel Castro with only the failing marijuana market for income. Or—and the colonel feared this more—North American antidrug agents or agents for competing syndicates might somehow gain information on his operations by posing as suppliers.

He countered this threat through innovation. Decades earlier he had experimented with opium production. Though the poppies did grow and did produce opium, he did not pursue opium production because marijuana proved to be a superior crop. He resumed his cultivation of opium. He also sent his men into the Andes to gather thousands of coca seeds and bushes.

Experts told him coca required the cool, high-altitude climate of the Andes to grow. Textbooks stated that coca withered in temperate or humid climates. The colonel did what others assumed to be impossible. Prior to the cocaine craze, Peru and Bolivia and a few areas of Colombia had produced the world's supply of the drug. There had been no need to plant in other regions. Therefore, no one had planted coca outside the Andes. But the colonel proved that not only could coca grow in the low-altitude heat and humidity of the jungle, but that coca flourished.

The colonel's secret cultivation of coca eliminated the weak link in his syndicate. Now his plantations supplied all the raw coca for his laboratories. When governments changed in Peru and Bolivia and the new administrations cooperated with the antidrug campaigns of the North Americans, rival syndicates suffered attacks and arrests and the cutoff of raw coca paste. But the colonel's operations continued untouched. The international law-enforcement campaigns against the cocaine trade only increased the price North Americans and Europeans would pay for cocaine they smoked or snorted or injected.

Throughout his life Colonel Castro had conquered opposition and profited from change. He had met every challenge. His wealth and power increased by the year. But now, in his middle age, he feared the future because he doubted the abilities of his son, Enrique.

Could Enrique equal the achievements of his father and grandfather? Could he meet the challenges of the future, when his father could not guide him?

The answers to his questions, like the future, remained unknown.

7

"You've gone crazy! Out of your heads! You think you'll just waltz into Colombia and do your find-and-kill number? Alone, without backup?"

Davis stared at the three men of Able Team, his eyes going from one man to the next. Behind him, the late-afternoon sun blazed horizontally through the Lear's ports. At ten the previous evening, he had piloted the jet from San Diego. They stopped at Mazatlán to pick up Blancanales and refuel. Landing again in the Canal Zone, Davis refueled a second time. But he refused to continue the flight without knowing the destination. When they told him Colombia, he could not believe them.

"Just fly the plane," Lyons told him. "We don't need you giving us mission evaluations."

"Hey," Davis snapped back, "I'm on your side. I wouldn't have agreed on this 'destination unknown' flight plan unless I was on your side. Now hear me. Colombia is a very difficult place to operate. The government works for the dope syndicates. The army works for the dope syndicates. The guerrillas work for the dope syndicates. Nothing in that country is straight. Even the DEA operations get twisted. Times that we figured we've scored against the syndicate, burning plantations, wiping out labs, putting mobsters away, it turns out that one syndicate has used us against another, maneuvered the agency into using U.S. personnel and planes to pull a strike on their competitors. They don't call that place 'Cacabia' for nothing. It'll make that time in Mexico look like an afternoon of miniature golf. Why didn't you at least let me set up some contacts for you?''

Blancanales glanced at his partners before answering. He silenced Lyons with a raised hand. "Don't be rude. The man's on our side, he's proved that. Davis, thank you for offering, but you know the problem—"

"Yeah, the problem!" Lyons interrupted. "We don't want to get shot down again. We don't want goons waiting for us when we get off the plane."

"We can trust you," Blancanales continued. "But you know that going into a liaison arrangement with the agency creates security problems..." he said, letting his voice trail off.

"Those problems got fixed," Davis countered.

"Perhaps. And perhaps not. We knew we could trust you to pilot a plane and not report our destination to anyone else in the agency. However, we want our agency involvement to end with you. We can't risk trusting anyone else."

"Oh, man!" Davis paced the aisle, running one hand through his short-cut hair. He spun around. "You're not hearing me! You will not be able to operate. That gear you've got," he said, pointing to the large shipping crates at the back of the plane. "You can't fake out the syndicates by marking the cases Cameras, Recorders, Film. You can't fake them out by telling them you're newsmen working on a story."

"Why not?" Gadgets asked. "Don't you watch television? News crews go everywhere."

"Not to Colombia! Not into the mountains! Not into syndicate territory! You won't get out of Bogotá. At the first checkpoint, you go straight to prison. You won't even get that far. You try to rent—or steal, whatever—a car, the informers will set you up."

"And forget where you went," Gadgets added.

"Just fly the plane," Lyons told him again. "Once we get there, all we want you to do is turn around and go home."

"And leave you know-it-all specialists to get yourselves killed." Davis shook his head as he returned to the pilot's cabin. "What a waste."

Able Team waited until Davis shut the compartment door before continuing their discussion. Lyons turned the map of Medellín faceup and pointed to the airport outside the city. "We'll have a few hours before Castro's plane comes in. By that time, we'll have rented cars, just like any tourist, and be ready to go."

Chandler looked at the closed door to the pilot's compartment. The prosecutor had remained silent throughout the argument in diffidence to the three "dirty war" veterans, but now he spoke. "He's right. We won't be able to operate."

"Prosecutor," Gadgets jived, "we do this all the time. We got the tricks down, man. Down!"

"I believe you. But you said yourselves Colombia's new to you. In the course of my investigations, I have worked with several agents who worked in Colombia. It's exactly like what the pilot said. The dope syndicates even have their own political party. I don't believe you should assume we can operate as free agents. There are too many uncertainties."

"Like what?" Lyons demanded.

"We've assumed that Castro will lead us to the gang. What if they off him at the airport? They could. He's a screw up. Why should they give a screw up courier another chance?"

"He's not a courier," Lyons countered. "And I don't think they'll kill him. Why did the big time attorney—that one from Washington?"

"Smithson?"

"Yeah, him. Why would he fly to California? Why did the gang fly Castro back to Colombia?"

"I can think of several reasons. Number one, if they killed him in the U.S. they would give us another chance at the gang. Number two, if he thought they intended to execute him, he might go state's witness. But in Colombia they could have twenty different gunmen do the killing. No chance of failure."

"Then we'll take one of the goons that kill him," Lyons explained. "He'll lead us back to the gang. We have to stay flexible with our planning. Otherwise we can't respond to the situation as it develops."

"And what if they have the police or the army kill him? They won't even know who set Castro up. Just a name and face. Number three, what if he isn't a courier? What if he's got enough rank in the organization to merit a plane ride away from the airport? Your planning doesn't meet that contingency.

Even if we rent a plane, how can we follow another plane?''

"True," Blancanales agreed.

"We'll work that out on the ground."

"Four strangers?" Chandler asked, incredulous. "Three of them Anglo? And number four—this one's unlikely, but possible—what if Enrique Castro's involved with the Castro family down here? There's a Colonel Castro who commands an army battalion and he's rumored to be involved in drugs. Castro's a common name and I don't believe anyone related to a gang leader would actually touch drugs, not when they could hire couriers, but what if he is? That could explain why Smithson flew out from Washington."

"Why didn't you raise these objections before?" Blancanales asked. "We've been talking for hours about this."

"Because I assumed you three had at least some contacts down there. You three are the heavies. I'm just a lightweight paper pusher. You had all the moves down. You had a contact for the information on the Route Five investigation. You had a contact for all that equipment and weapons back there. You had a contact for this plane and the pilot. But you never said we'd be going in alone."

"But we're not," Lyons said, grinning. "We're taking you. You know all about the syndicates."

"I don't know that much about Route Five. Nobody does. It's a closed gang. I know how it distributes in the U.S. I know how it interlinks with the transnational banking corporations. But that won't help us in the mountains. You've got to get someone who knows the local territory."

Lyons shook his head.

AFTER ANNOUNCING HIS LANDING as a fueling stop, Davis received clearance from the Colombian flight controllers. He guided the Lear through the clouds. At ten thousand feet he saw Medellín. Like a cloth of stars, the lights of the old colonial city spread across the mountains. But beyond the lights Davis saw only the unbroken darkness of wilderness, a darkness that concealed an underworld of corrupt government officials, a national army commanded by gangsters, transnational drug syndicates and private gangs with modern weapons.

"Those guys are crazy," Davis muttered to himself.

Minutes later, after a perfect landing, the Lear jet taxied to the refueling stations. Davis watched the facilities of the airport pass. Past the commercial section, he saw hangars housing expensive commuter jets.

And cargo planes. Maintenance crews serviced and fueled planes that had once shuttled passengers from country to country. He saw several models of long-distance passenger planes, and every one had been converted to carry cargo.

A field man with two red-coned flashlights signaled Davis to turn the Lear. Touching the brakes, Davis eased the jet through a slow left. He saw other planes in the refueling area. The field man signaled Davis to cut the engines.

Behind him, he heard Able Team talking in the

cabin. Sometime during the refueling, they would jump out of the plane and slip away. Davis looked around. He saw a few field men a hundred yards away. Other technicians worked in the hangars. It looked as if the "specialists" would be able to make their break. But what then?

His attention was drawn to a distant hangar, where technicians polished a Huey. Painted sky blue, marked with the insignia of the Colombian Ministry of the Interior, the helicopter had been one of the many supplied to Colombia to fight the war against drugs.

It was exactly what the specialists needed. Davis thought about letting Able Team and the new guy slip away. Four North Americans operating alone in Cacalombia, the country of shit. Up against everything a corrupt government, a corrupt army, and all that the hundreds of gangs could hit them with.

He did not want another adventure. He did not want to fly around in the Andes in another stolen helicopter. He did not want to risk his career helping those specialists again. Mexico had been different. His superiors accepted his story of the crash, of stealing the helicopter from the phony Mexican army unit, of flying across Mexico to attack a syndicate in the highrise corporate towers of Mexico City. But this time?

An unauthorized flight to an unauthorized destination and the theft of another government's aircraft.

Unemployment. Maybe a federal prison if he was lucky. If he was unlucky, a Colombian prison, where certain death awaited him when the other inmates learned he worked for the DEA.

But if he didn't help, those three good men and the prosecutor would die. The best death they could hope for would be a quick bullet in a firefight. Davis had seen the black-and-white photos of what the Colombian syndicates did to informers and cops. A bullet in the brain would be good luck.

If he didn't pilot another Huey, in another adventure, those four Americans wouldn't come back.

"Damn it!" Davis cursed. "Those goddamned arrogant, spaced-out shock troopers. Can't even admit they need help."

Leaving his seat, Davis threw open the compartment door. The four men looked up from their gear as he entered. The blond one—the one called Ironman because he could run forever—pointed back to the pilot's compartment.

"Just wait, Davis. We'll be gone in a few minutes. We'll get our transportation and be on our way."

Then Davis pointed and said, "Look out there. Look! What do you see? You see that helicopter?"

"That blue one?" the Wizard asked. "What about it?"

"That's your transportation. And I'll be flying it!"

IN THE DAY-GLO YELLOW RAIN SLICKER of a field man, Blancanales stood near one of the passenger loading bridges outside the terminal. He stayed in the shadows, watching the other workers. Under the plastic-and-foam ear protectors he wore, Davis's voice came to him through his hand radio's earphone. In the Lear, the pilot monitored the conversations between the flight controllers and the approaching planes.

"They've announced the arrival of the flight," Davis told him. "You should see it touching down now."

Across the colored lights of the runways, Blancanales saw the wing lights of a jetliner descending from the darkness. The field men also saw the plane arrive. Drivers positioned their service vehicles. Technicians stood by with their equipment. Two workers stood at wide doors leading to the luggage conveyor. Above him, Blancanales saw other workers standing at the accordian-folded flex-link that would clamp over the jetliner's exit.

Everyone waited for the jetliner to taxi into position.

High beams flashing, a crew van sped across the apron. The waiting workers watched the van weave past trucks and luggage trailers.

The van stopped near the ramp and two square-faced men in dark suits stepped out. Both men held the pistol grips of the Uzi submachine guns slung from their shoulders. Inside, another man remained seated. The workers looked away, carefully ignoring the van and the men.

Blancanales took two steps back before speaking into his hand radio. "A crew van just pulled up. Two heavies with Uzis got out. They're waiting for the plane."

"A bright orange van? With three men inside, besides the driver?"

"That's it."

"It just left one of the hangars over here."

"Here comes the jet . . . put the prosecutor on."

"Here I am," Chandler told him.

"Hold on. The plane's coming up to unload. I'm moving up on the van."

Pocketing the radio, Blancanales left the shadows. The field men snapped into their duties as a tug truck pulled the jetliner to the passenger bridge. Blancanales continued along the bridge to stand next to a catering truck. He had an unobstructed view of the van. He memorized the features of the gunmen.

Above him, the airliner's side exit opened. A stewardess looked out, then technicians clamped the flex-link to the side of the airliner. One of the gunmen leaned into the van.

Blancanales waited, watching the gunmen. A minute later, one of the passenger ramp's side doors opened. Blancanales saw Enrique Raul Castro hurry down the aluminum stairs.

A man stepped out of the crew van. The gunmen gripped their weapons, their eyes scanning the activity around them. Behind them, the short, broad-shouldered man watched Castro come down the stairs. Blancanales studied the middle-aged man, memorizing his features, clothing and mannerisms. The man wore a perfectly tailored business suit. His shoes gleamed. Light flashed from the precious stones of his rings as he raised his arms to greet the murderer Castro.

As the two men embraced, Blancanales slipped away. He had seen enough. Though the roar of the jets had blasted away the older man's words, Blancanales had read his lips as he embraced Castro.

"My son, my son...."

Enrique Raul Castro had returned home to his father, Colonel José Alvarado Castro.

8

As the light plane bucked high-altitude turbulence, the pilot jerked and wrenched the control yoke to maintain his compass bearing. He flew blind through the night, guiding the plane by instruments. A wide-shouldered bodyguard sat in the copilot's seat monitoring the battalion frequency. In the back of the passenger compartment, Colonel Castro listened to his son's explanation of his arrest in the United States.

"It was bad luck," Enrique stated. "Only that and nothing else. The courier could not make the pickup. It was an easy job, so I did it. No one is ever on that beach at night. Except for that stupid lifeguard, there would have been no problem. He wanted to give me a ticket for fishing at night. Stupid! And then that woman and the girl. Sleeping on the beach! How could that be anything but luck, two women sleeping on a beach in California where no one sleeps on the beaches. That one beach. Impossible luck!"

"That is why we have couriers," the colonel told him. "In case of bad luck...."

"But I am free now. So it is all of no consequence," Enrique said with a shrug.

"No consequence!" his father shouted. "They

know your face and your business. They will be waiting for you to make another mistake.''

"I made no mistakes.''

"Then why were you arrested? You made a mistake handling the stuff yourself. You are my son, you do not need to do the work of a courier. What if my lawyers had not freed you? What if you were in a prison now? Waiting to be executed?''

Enrique dismissed that idea with a laugh. "You would not allow that.''

"My power has limits.''

"Your money doesn't.''

"Boy, what is in your mind? Do you think I operate like some American tourist? 'I want this, I want that, here is the money'? After all these years working with me, all the deals, all the politics, you say that?''

"Your money paid the lawyers.''

"And my money goes to the politicians and the police and all the other whores in the line. But money buys only so much. There are some men who cannot be bought and that is why you went to court.''

Pointing his index finger like the barrel of a pistol, Enrique made two popping sounds. "What money cannot buy, the gun can fix.''

"Boy, boy, boy, why have you not learned?''

"Don't call me boy! I am a man!''

"Then act like a man! You talk like a girl with a rich father—''

"Colonel!'' The bodyguard turned to face his commander. "There is an attack on the estate!''

The man turned up the volume of the radio monitor. Scratchy with static, the frequency carried panicky voices talking over one another in an incomprehensible confusion of transmissions. One voice spoke again and again, repeating a command for calm.

"That is Captain Munoz," the colonel said.

They listened as the officer finally restored order on the frequency. He requested one outpost to report. The words came in a static-distorted rush. But they recognized one word that the outpost radio operator repeated: "Guajiros! Guajiros!"

A LIGHT RAIN FELL on Medellín, blurring the brilliant lights of the runways and hangars. Now, only two hours before dawn, the airport activity slowed. Flights touched down infrequently. Workers stayed in the warmth of the terminals and hangars unless their duties demanded that they step into the chill night.

Blancanales moved toward the hangar housing the Colombian government helicopter. He still wore the Day-Glo yellow rain slicker he had stolen hours before. But under the slicker, he now wore black slacks and a black turtleneck sweater. In one pocket, he had a black ski mask.

A hundred yards away, a soldier waved a flashlight along the side of a hangar. The soldier continued along the front of the building, then checked the opposite wall before continuing on to the next hangar in the row. Blancanales watched the soldier. As the sentry checked a doorway, Blancanales stepped between two parked trucks.

He keyed his hand radio. "Going in," he whispered.

Slipping off the plastic rain slicker, he rolled it into a tight bundle and jammed it under his belt. He pulled his black sweater over the roll of brilliant yellow plastic. Then he pulled the black ski mask down over his face and neck.

Only a shadow within the darkness, he dashed from the parked trucks to one of the side doors of the hangar. He stood at the corrugated-aluminum door a moment, listening. Nothing moved inside.

He waited, listening. Finally the whine of a jet's engines came from across the airport. Blancanales stuck the blade of the electric lock pick into the keyhole.

The device vibrated at thousands of cycles per second, jittering the lock's pins through hundreds of thousands of positions as Blancanales tried to turn the handle. The distant engine noise covered the humming resonating from the metal door.

After a few seconds the random patterns of the moving pins finally passed through the pattern formed by the proper key. The lock opened, and Blancanales pulled back the door and slipped into the darkness of the hangar. He checked the inside lock mechanism and set it to remain unlocked. Then he eased the door closed. Crouching in the darkness, he keyed his radio again.

"I'm in," he said.

"On our way," Lyons replied.

Motionless for minutes, Blancanales waited, listening, his eyes sweeping the darkness. The door beside him opened. Lyons and Davis rushed into the hangar.

"Any problems?" he asked them.

"Nothing—"

"Down!"

They crouched against the workbenches as the beam of a flashlight swept across the windows set in the aircraft doors of the hangar. The sound of the sentry's footsteps passed.

"Close," Davis whispered.

"Makes it exciting," Lyons countered. "Now go hotwire that helicopter."

Lyons and Blancanales took positions in the front of the hangar. Though they had only a limited field of vision, they heard every movement. Somewhere outside, they heard voices as sentries greeted one another.

Behind them, Davis opened the doors of the helicopter and checked the instruments with a penlight. Then he turned his back to the doors and read the maintenance log of the helicopter.

"Cherry. . . ."

"Quiet!" Lyons said.

"Can you take it?" Blancanales whispered.

"Sure can. Signal for that distraction."

Blancanales keyed his radio and spoke quickly. "Wizard. We're ready. Do your trick."

"Pushing the button. . . ." the reply came back.

On the far side of the hangar area, a radio-triggered fuse popped, initiating the explosive charge of a miniature MU-50G controlled-effect grenade. The tiny grenade, designed for the close-quarter combat of antiterrorist actions, had a forty-six gram charge of TNT to propel fourteen hundred steel balls. The reduced charge of explosive limited the one hundred percent kill diameter to ten yards.

However, the exploding grenade injured no one. Blancanales had jammed the grenade and radio detonator between the rear axle and gas tank of a truck. Steel balls punched hundreds of pinholes through the thin sheet metal of the gas tank, the blast spraying gasoline.

Flame flashed into the night.

In the darkness of the hangar, the three men waited as an orange glow lit the misting rain. Sentries ran past the hangar. Lyons and Blancanales waited. A siren sounded. Their hand radios buzzed.

"The gang's all there," Gadgets told his partners.

Lyons and Blancanales ran to the Huey. Davis took his place in the pilot's seat as they pushed the helicopter toward the doors. In the sheet-metal hangar, the rollers on the skids squealed and clicked, reverberating in the cavernous interior.

Rushing to the doors, Blancanales threw aside the heavy latch. He pushed one door to the side while Lyons shoved the other away. Outside, fire lit the overcast sky. They saw no one in the wide expanse of rain-glistening tarmac in front of the row of hangars.

But they took no chances. Jerking out the pins on CS-CN grenades, they threw the grenades in opposite directions. The canisters clanked as they bounced over the asphalt. Then they threw smoke grenades.

A screen of smoke and chemicals obscured each end of the corridor between the hangars. Returning to the Huey, the two men pushed the helicopter clear of the hangar.

Davis initiated the electric starter, the whine of the engine pierced the air like another siren. The rotors turned. Then the turbine hissed as kerosene burned. The rotors spun to a blur.

A guard shouted. Lyons answered him with a CS-CN grenade. Blancanales threw another smoke bomb.

"Get in!" Davis shouted over the rotorthrob.

Lyons and Blancanales jumped through the side door and the asphalt fell away. Below, they saw figures running through the multicolored swirls of smoke. The hangars and runways tilted as Davis took the helicopter across the airport to where they had left the DEA jet.

Gadgets waved a flashlight. Dropping fast, Davis bounced the Huey on its skids. Immediately, Gadgets and Chandler heaved the shipping trunks and suitcases to the two men inside the converted troopship.

Headlights swept across the rows of parked planes as a vehicle raced toward the stolen helicopter. Chandler shoved the last trunk through the side door and climbed inside.

"Up, ace!" Gadgets shouted to Davis. "Take it up!"

Lights streaked beneath them as the helicopter gained speed, then they left the airport behind. Lyons threw the side door closed.

"The way you guys operate!" Chandler shouted. "Too much!"

"What do you mean?"

"Illegal entry into a foreign country! Arms smuggling! Theft of a million-dollar aircraft! Wild, man, wild!"

Lyons laughed. "Standard operating procedure."

9

Colonel Castro scanned the horizon with binoculars. Against a horizon bluing with dawn, a column of black smoke rose from the dark jungle. He leaned over the shoulder of the helicopter pilot and held the field-of-view on the rising smoke. Despite the rotor vibration jittering his hands, he saw a pinpoint of orange. The orange point flared from the darkness, becoming a flame, then died down. An instant later, another flame appeared.

El Cristal burned.

Hours before, as he flew from Medellín with his son, the alarm had come over the battalion frequency. He followed the battle on the radio, listening to men shout alarms, begging for reinforcements. Then finally—and suddenly—silence descended as the Guajiros exterminated the last defenders. By the time Castro's plane had arrived at his battalion's airfield, the voices of other soldiers spoke code phrases on the radio. Those soldiers advanced slowly, cautiously encircling the El Cristal processing-and-transportation complex, aware that the Guajiros might be waiting in ambush for the reinforcements.

But the reports from the first units entering El Cristal reported only death and ruins.

Now Colonel Castro flew to view the scene himself. He had left his son to pout at the mansion. He did not need Enrique angering him on this flight with his talk of luck and money and killing. True, the Castros had created their empire by exploiting luck, wealth and violence, but only when intelligence and calculation did not meet the challenge. If the colonel could believe what his impetuous young son had told him, Enrique would depend on corruption and terror in his operations. And blame his reversals on bad luck. Bad luck! The boy had made his own disaster and he called it bad luck. The colonel could not allow his son to continue with those conceptions.

Corruption and terror. . . like the Guajiros.

Animals! Those subhuman goons from the swamps of the north. The Guajiros took their name from Colombia's northernmost province, Guajira, a territory of lowlands along the Caribbean coast. Since pre-Colombian times, the inhabitants of the region had terrorized the other peoples of Colombia. Cannibal Caribe tribes preyed on Incan and Mayan travelers, later the Spanish and other European looters converging on the wealth of the New World. The Guajiros had continued in their barbaric isolation throughout the centuries, feared and loathed, the issue of indigenous Caribes interbreeding with Englishmen and escaped slaves, creating a race that good Colombians considered bestial and disgusting.

In the past few decades, as the marijuana plantations brought thousands of ships to the Guajira coast, groups of local criminals joined the international smuggling gangs in the illegal trade. The temporary alliances disintegrated as the local gangs murdered the outsiders. New gangs emerged, called Guajiros, and distinguished themselves from all the others with their absolute disregard for limits when it came to violence and greed.

Even the other gangsters recoiled from the horrors inflicted by the Guajiros. To stop a competitor, the army or the other established groups shot a few couriers. Rarely did the organized syndicates immediately employ terror, preferring to intimidate or co-opt before murdering their equals. But the Guajiros went directly to the home of the gang leader and slaughtered every man, woman and child in the household. The Guajiros pursued their competitors with a savage bloodlust that forced competing gangs to abandon their own vendettas and unite in syndicates for mutual defense.

The syndicates of Colombian army officers and gangsters made wealthy by the drug trade referred to themselves as the White Mafia. They called the Guajiros, for reason of their terror as well as their mixed ancestry, the Black Mafia.

Colonel Castro had fought the Guajiros often, on the open seas of the Caribbean, in the coastal ports, in the streets of Medellín, in the mountains and valleys of the wilderness. His soldiers were always on alert for Guajiro gangs trying to raid the plantations in the vast territory of Colonel Castro. In the northern ports along the Guajira peninsula, the savages had murdered men and stolen a few boatloads of drugs, but never had a major attack on the "white" syndicates operating in the Magdalena succeeded.

But during the night, Guajiros had looted and destroyed El Cristal.

From the thousand yard vantage of the hovering helicopter, Colonel Castro looked down at the smoking wreckage that had been a multimillion-dollar installation. Only ashes and concrete foundations remained of the laboratory and coca warehouses. Fire consumed the barracks and offices. In the smoking ruins of the hangars, the hulks of aircraft still glowed with the sparks of burning magnesium.

The colonel motioned for his aide to pass him the radio's microphone. He took the microphone and spoke with the officer on the ground. "Is the area secure?"

"None of them remain, Colonel. We believe they have been gone for hours."

"Did you find any of the attackers' bodies?"

"None. There was blood, but they left none of their dead."

"I will direct the pilot to land on the airstrip. Meet me there."

A minute later, the colonel stepped from the helicopter. The Colombian army captain leading the response unit stood to attention and saluted his commander.

"Where are the men who survived?" the colonel asked.

"There were only two, Colonel," the captain answered. He pointed across an equipment yard to a group of soldiers. "My medics—"

"Only two?"

"We searched and found no others. Come, they wait for your questions."

Vehicles still smoldered in the equipment yard. Cars and trucks had burned to blackened hulks. The two officers walked around one fire, clouds of choking black smoke drifting over them. The moist dawn air stank of incinerated plastic and scorched rubber.

Colonel Castro noticed the hundreds of cartridge casings littering the asphalt. He paused to pick up one.

"From Kalashnikov rifles," the captain told him.

A glance confirmed the information. Unlike most rifle cartridges, the 7.62mm x 39mm Kalashnikov cartridge did not produce high combustion pressures. This allowed ComBloc ammunition manufacturers to use cheap low-grade steel instead of brass as a casing metal. The cartridge casing Colonel Castro held had been manufactured of steel, then lacquered to prevent corrosion. Reading the end stamp, he saw the Cyrillic letters of the Russian alphabet.

"Guerrillas. . ." Castro began.

"Perhaps, Colonel. But the Communists sell their weapons to whoever has the money. The Guajiros also used American and European weapons."

The colonel picked up a brass casing. He read the letters PMC 9MM, identifying the cartridge as manufactured in South Korea. The colonel's forces used 9mm ammunition manufactured in Argentina. "Correct. We cannot assume they were a guerrilla gang."

Continuing a few more steps, the colonel saw the first dead soldier. The man had died as he fired from behind the shelter of a pallet-load of compressed burlap sacks. Not content with killing the defender, the Guajiros had hacked the body with machetes, severing the head and hands and opening the torso to thousands of green-back flies. The colonel paused for a moment to study the savagery, then continued.

"The animals . . ." he muttered.

"They did that to all the men they found. The dead and the living," the corporal added.

The group of radiomen and medics turned and saluted as their commander approached. The two wounded soldiers started to rise to their feet, but Colonel Castro motioned for them to stay down.

One man had suffered a superficial bullet wound to the side of his head. Waving away flies, the medic placed a field dressing over the bloody gouge. The other soldier grimaced with the pain of a bullet-shattered arm. Crouching beside the men, the colonel noted that both had only empty pouches on the ammunition bandoliers.

"What happened?" Colonel Castro asked them.

"They came in a plane," the bullet-grazed soldier answered. "We were standing sentry at the end of the airstrip, down there—" The soldier pointed to the green wall of jungle a thousand yards away from the processing complex. "We had been told a plane would come in during the night. I heard the plane. The runway lights came on. The plane landed—"

"Did you see the type of plane?"

"A big one. But only two engines. I think it was a DC-3."

"Propellers or jet?"

"Propellers. I am sure; I saw them spinning."

"Markings?"

"I am sorry, but I did not see. It was dark and the distance was too far."

"Continue."

"Then shooting started. A storm of shooting without stop. My walkie-talkie said that commandos had attacked. We took cover and fired at the plane. Machine guns and rifles fired at us and a bullet hit me. I moved and continued firing, moving and shooting until I ran out of ammunition. When the plane flew away, I had only my pistol and I fired at the plane, but I don't think I hit it."

"Very good. You did your duty. And you, my soldier? What can you tell me?"

In great pain, the soldier answered, speaking slowly. "When the machine gun hit him, he went out cold. I saw his head bleeding, I thought he was dead. I started for the base, then I saw them in the lights and I shot as I continued through the brush and trees. But then I was hit and I could not move. The soldiers found me and carried me here this morning...."

"What did you see of the Guajiros?"

"Only...only forms...I did not get close."

"Uniforms? Their clothing?"

"I am sorry, Colonel, but I did not get close enough...the machine guns...."

"You were very brave. You did the best you could. Thank you. The battalion is fortunate to have soldiers of your courage. Come to me for reassignment when your arm heals. Both of you."

Colonel Castro left the group of soldiers. He mentally reviewed the very limited information he had gained from the wounded sentries. What they had told him explained the casings everywhere. To hit two soldiers, in the night, firing from hundreds of yards away required extravagant expenditure of ammunition. The raiders obviously came prepared to overwhelm any defensive force.

The aircraft employed in the attack remained unknown. Though the plane could have been an old DC-3, some of the Guajiro gangs had hijacked or purchased the latest models of short-range transports. The aircraft might identify the gang. The colonel would send his service technicians to examine the runway pavement for any clues as to the manufacturer or model of the raiders' plane—patterns of skid marks, tire tracks, fluid leaks, anything.

As he considered the mystery and how to solve it— spies, informers, government air-traffic records—the colonel surveyed the devastated complex. In addition to the cocaine stolen—worth ten million dollars delivered to a buyer in Miami, thirty to forty million on the streets—the raiders had destroyed an installation that had cost the colonel millions of dollars. And the colonel would also lose months of production while he rebuilt the laboratories, warehouses and aircraft hangars.

If he rebuilt the complex. The Guajiros knew its location. If he rebuilt the laboratory and returned the complex to production, the Guajiros would raid again in the future. But then again, he had many other labs and airfields scattered throughout his lands, and men harvesting and refining the coca crops. Colonel Castro could not simply move the laboratory to another location and expect the facility to be secure.

No, security—and honor—dictated a military response to this raid. Unless he destroyed the Guajiro gang responsible, his other processing centers faced attack and destruction.

But first he must identify the particular gang responsible, the one that had dared to directly confront his power and authority. If he attacked the Guajiro syndicates indiscriminately, he would start a war between the underworld factions of Colombia. For that reason, the "white" syndicates allied with Colonel Castro would not support an unfocused campaign of revenge against the Guajiros.

How could he identify the raiders?

Infiltration and observation.

A Guajiro gang now had ten million dollars' worth of pure crystalline cocaine to sell.

The colonel's syndicate employed a few North Americans in sensitive positions throughout Colombia. They played the roles of multinational corporation executives and employees. Some of the North Americans never touched cocaine or associated with traffickers. Others increased their company income by buying and selling cocaine. All of the men served Colonel Castro.

He would call those men together, brief them and dispatch them north to the ports of the Guajira peninsula. He would also order his men to study whatever evidence remained on the scene of the raid.

And he would order a general security alert at all his facilities everywhere on the *finca*.

10

Slashing branches, the stolen helicopter dropped into the clearing. Chandler looked out through the side door at the shadowy green of the dawn jungle. A vivid red-and-blue bird flapped into the rotor blades, dying in an explosion of feathers.

Beside Chandler the three men of Able Team were snapping back the actuators of their automatic rifles. They wore web gear and bandoliers of magazines over their sports coats and slacks. Chandler jammed a magazine into his M-16 but did not chamber a round. Almost fifteen years had passed since he used an M-16, and he did not want an accidental discharge. He gripped the weapon, waiting, watching the wall of trees and flowering vines, his heart beating as fast as it had the first time he had dropped into an unsecured landing zone.

He heard a snap. A bullet? A broken rotor? Panicking, Chandler turned to the others.

Gadgets picked a pink film of bubble gum off his face.

The skids touched the ground. The rotor speed dropped as Davis eased back on the power. He leaned back from the pilot's chair and shouted, "Check it out!"

Lyons and Gadgets threw open the side doors. They signaled for Blancanales and Chandler to cover them, then stepped into a waist-high tangle of lush green vegetation. Chandler finally pulled back and released the actuator of his M-16 to strip a cartridge off the magazine. He kept the muzzle of the rifle up, his thumb on the safety-fire-selector as he scanned the jungle, his eyes pausing on every shadow.

Gadgets thrashed through the tangled undergrowth for a few steps then reached the trees. He cut to his right, checking the perimeter of the clearing, his head swiveling from side to side. Sometimes he stopped to look at the ground. He stood still for a moment, looking in all directions, then stepped into the darkness of the trees.

A flight of small birds flashed from above, their yellow wings and red cowls like flames. Chandler waited for Gadgets to step out of the jungle. A minute passed. Lyons returned to the helicopter.

"It's clear," he shouted. "No one's been here lately. Davis! Kill the engine!"

Chandler pointed to the jungle. "The Wizard went in there. And he hasn't come out."

"Buzz him. Use your radio." Lyons stripped off his coat and shirt. He put on a black fatigue shirt. He buckled his web gear over the shirt, then found his dark fatigue pants and black nylon jungle boots in his shipping trunk.

Pressing down the transmit key of the unfamiliar high-tech walkie-talkie, Chandler said, "Calling the Wizard. Where are you?"

No answer.

"Wizard! What's going on? Answer if you can."

A few seconds passed before Gadgets finally replied. "Give me two minutes slack, will you? I'm taking a shit."

"Oh, yeah, uh...sure. Just didn't know what...."

"Now you do."

The turbine roar quit. Above them, the rotors slowed, cutting the air in slower and slower turns. Then silence descended. For the two hours of the flight from Medellín, they had endured the rotor-throb and vibration of the helicopter. Now, the silence seemed absolute. But then the small sounds of the jungle returned.

Birds cried out. A macaw squawked and flew past the helicopter. Chandler heard the macaw's wings flapping the air. He looked around at the rampant fertility. He saw walls of trees and vines around the overgrown clearing. Hanging chains of orchids splashed colors on the green. Above him, the rectangle of overarching branches was glowing luminescent green with dawn light.

Then he noticed the vegetation around him. Though he saw several varieties of ferns and flowering tropical plants, the dominant plant had wide, handlike clusters of five and seven bladed leaves.

Cannabis sativa. Marijuana. Everywhere. Glistening with dew. The leaves and branches grew in tangles to almost waist height. Dopers had once farmed this clearing but, judging from the way the jungle had reclaimed the clearing, had abandoned it sometime in the past year. Discounting for water content, Chandler saw perhaps a hundred kilos of immature marijuana in the clearing. Abandoned to the jungle.

This is not San Diego, Chandler thought. I am in a different country now.

"Hey, Prosecutor!" The blond, hard-muscled specialist he knew only as the Ironman interrupted his daydreaming. "Don't just sit there sightseeing and grinning. Get into your fatigues. Those slacks and white shirt are not proper attire for this particular case."

"Oh, yeah. Okay. Say, Ironman, you know what's growing here? It's dope—"

He felt his hand radio click, one-two-three, the three-click code repeating again and again. Lyons dropped to a crouch, Blancanales moving in a blur. Barefooted, his boots in his hands, Lyons went low in the grass. He frantically pulled on the boots and whipped the laces from side to side.

Still sitting in the side door, Chandler heard the noise of men thrashing through the brush. Metal banged on metal. Then a voice called out in Spanish. *"¿Que es la problema con su coptero?"*

Chandler stared at the line of camouflage-uniformed soldiers walking from the trees. All carried autoweapons, the rifles and Uzi submachine guns hanging from slings at a comfortable gut-high position. As the line of soldiers approached the helicopter, the lead man called out, *"Y porque ustedes viennen—"*

The patrol leader saw Chandler's Anglo features. Startling, he swung up the muzzle of his Uzi. He never completed the motion.

Autofire blasted the silence, high-velocity slugs striking the line of men from the side, blood exploding from their uniforms, men lurching with impacts, others spinning to fire at the unseen rifleman.

Then autofire exploded from the ground and chopped flowers and marijuana flew up. The line of men was thrown back, their faces and chests suddenly spotted with blood.

Chandler raised his rifle. As if in a dream, he pointed the M-16 at the group of dead and dying men and pulled the trigger. But his rifle did not fire. He jerked the trigger again and again.

The one-sided firefight had ended. Lyons rose from the earth in a rush and charged the sprawled soldiers. Chandler saw Lyons pointing his autoweapon at the men. Then Blancanales thrashed past Lyons and took cover in the trees.

In the silence, his hands shaking, Chandler fumbled with his rifle. He slammed the forward-assist plunger with the heel of his hand and the magazine fell out of its well. Kneeling down, he found the magazine and jammed it back into the rifle. He slapped the base of the magazine and snapped back the actuator again.

A burst ripped the silence as he fired straight up into the sky. Behind him somewhere in the ferns, Davis called out, "Where are they? Did you hit them?"

"Hit who?" Chandler asked.

"The soldiers!"

"They're dead!"

"Then who are you shooting at?"

On the floor of the helicopter, his hand radio

buzzed. He heard the Ironman's voice. "Where are they coming from? How many?"

Setting his rifle's safety, Chandler grabbed the radio with his left hand. He stuttered out, "It was... it was an...accident, an accidental discharge. There aren't any more of the soldiers coming."

"Lawyer, get your act together."

He heard Davis laughing. Chandler went flat in the ferns and tangled marijuana until his pulse slowed. Then he rose to one knee so that he could scan the clearing. He saw no movement.

For minutes he knelt there, watching. On the other side of the helicopter, he heard Davis moving.

"Ah, goddamn it! Ants—ah, man!" The pilot thrashed and cursed, slapping at his body.

Chandler waited for the specialists to return. The birds sang again. Insects hummed around him. An iridescent blue butterfly fluttered past him, then returned and landed on the flash-suppressor of his M-16, opening and closing its wings against the black metal of the weapon.

His hand radio buzzed again. "Prosecutor here."

"Anything there?"

"Nothing."

"We're coming back."

A minute later Lyons and Gadgets emerged from the trees. Lyons stopped at the corpses. Gadgets thrashed through the ferns to Chandler. The Able Team electronics specialist wore a mass of interwoven marijuana branches as a hat. A garland of marijuana camouflage decorated his Colt Assault Rifle.

"So, Mr. Prosecutor...." Gadgets stopped to chuckle. "So what's the cloud body count?"

"Are you high on that stuff?"

"What? Me?"

"That's marijuana you're wearing. You smoking it, too?"

"Mr. Chandler, it isn't me," Gadgets said, tapping himself in the chest, "who's been shooting at the sky. It just so happens I've never had a hundred-dollar hat before. Don't you think I've got a hundred dollars' worth on my head? Makes for okay camouflage."

Despite his nervousness and embarrassment, Chandler laughed. Even Davis, sitting in the helicopter applying local anesthetic to the ant bites swelling his legs, laughed. Gadgets continued his jive.

"I mean, I'm squatting there and I look around and it's all over the place. I made myself this hat. And I used some for toilet paper, but that stuff I didn't tear off the plant. That branch is still growing. Next year, up in New York, some Jerseyboy will smoke his dope and say, 'Wow, heavy shit,' and you know, he just might be talking the truth."

They crouched beside the helicopter, laughing, Chandler the errant deputy district attorney and Gadgets Schwarz, the ex-Green Beret veteran of never-known wars on five continents. Lyons's shout stopped them.

"Prosecutor! That white shirt's a great target. Change into the fatigues. Wizard, come look at these soldiers."

Gadgets got serious. "Time to debrief the dead," he said as he started to move.

Lyons crouched among the corpses, emptying the patrol leader's pockets. He had found a wad of pages from a glossy magazine, a knife, a folded plastic-protected map, a plastic straw and a handworked snakeskin pouch heavy with crystalline cocaine.

Unfolding the map, they saw the whorls and lines of a topographic chart. On the other side, a large-scale map indicated roads and installations.

"We're in business," Lyons commented.

Gadgets freed a radio from a dead man. Examining the radio, he used a handful of marijuana to wipe blood from the case. Then he checked it for damage.

"Think they put out a message before they walked in on us?" Lyons asked his partner.

"Didn't see it. I watched them as they noticed the helicopter. Then they just walked in. Their officers won't know these losers are gone. And when they know the patrol's gone, no one will know where."

Lyons went from corpse to corpse, turning each over. "No unit identification, but military gear."

"Anyone can buy weapons and OD green fatigues."

"Private army?"

"Everyone's telling us how organized the gangs are, why not uniforms and gear for the goon squads?"

Chandler joined them. He wore camouflage fatigues and web gear new from the box. The fatigues still had creases in the pants and down the shirt's long sleeves. His regulation-issue .38-caliber Smith & Wesson revolver rode in a brown leather shoulder holster.

"Looking sharp, Lawyer," Gadgets jived. "Not like that ex-cop in the worn-out gook suit. It's not even black anymore."

Lyons ignored his partner's taunt. He turned to Chandler and said, "Forget that leather shoulder holster. Soon as the day heats up, you'll sweat, soak it and it'll start to rot. Won't last two days. There's a couple of nylon holsters on these losers. Strip one off."

"Oh, yeah. Good point," Chandler replied.

"And forget the revolver, too. Put it in your boot or somewhere as a backup, but take one of the auto-pistols. That guy over there, the one with three eyes. He's got a Colt Government Model."

"You recommend that pistol?"

"If you want to kill people. Here, look at this map. Is this town the one where you said the battalion is headquartered?"

"Colina Blanca," Chandler said as he nodded. "That's the garrison town. Supposedly old General Castro had one of his palaces there."

"Then that's where we're going."

Lyons called out to Davis. "Hey, flyboy. We didn't bring gear for you. Come over here and do your shopping."

As Davis and Chandler outfitted themselves with the dead men's equipment and uniforms, Able Team plotted the next move.

"We chance leaving the helicopter here?" Gadgets asked Lyons.

"We'd be taking a chance to move it now," Lyons responded. Keying his hand radio, he buzzed Blancanales. "Pol, we got a map. It squares with what the prosecutor told us about the Castro battalion."

"Then we know where we're going."

They took the next hour to bury the dead soldiers in the jungle, then camouflage the helicopter with a pile of branches and small trees.

Then the five Americans marched for the battalion headquarters of Colonel Castro.

11

"No investigation!" Enrique Raul Castro snapped. "Why bother? Are we police? Must we take evidence to a court? This is war and it must be fought as war!"

"You know nothing!" Colonel Castro shouted down his son. "Do not tell me what I must do."

They argued in the musty study that had been the favorite refuge of the general. Leather-bound volumes from Spain and colonial Mexico filled the shelves. Heavy hardwood furniture, crafted by *indigena* peons, polished by *indigena* maids for three generations, cluttered the room. The finish on the desk and chairs and tables was black with accumulated wax. Rotting burgundy velvet drapes blocked the searing equatorial sun.

To maintain a link with the past, the colonel maintained this one room of the mansion as his father had left it. His father's portrait hung on one wall, his scowling features darkened by exposure, scarred by smallpox and knives. The artist had captured the flame of the general's ego in his blazing eyes and the flashing gold of the medals on his severe uniform. The hard sneer of the old man's lips told of his cruelty.

"My son," the colonel continued after calming himself, "remember that I...our organization operates in alliance with many other organizations. Though we maintain absolutely independent production and distribution, we do not exist alone in Colombia or in the world. I cooperate with the leaders of many other organizations. Together, we maintain control over the business, the politicians and the foreigners. We maintain control because we conduct our affairs in a rational, methodical manner. To do as you want, I would violate the principles that govern the operations of our many syndicates—''

"But I have talked with all of them!" Enrique broke in as he paced the floor with the restless malevolence of a caged predator. "All the leaders hate the Guajiros. All the syndicates fight those black gangs. The attack was an affront to our honor! We must show ourselves to be the equal of all the others."

Colonel Castro glanced at the portrait of his father. The general had known the value of alliances and politics. He had acted alone only when he had no alternative. But now Enrique talked of war—war first, not war after the failure of intimidation, or assassination, or a plotted and carefully executed counterstrike. Not war with the backing of their allies.

War. Young men who have never fought wars declared war quickly, without thought. Enrique did not consider the cost in lives and money. Any action against the Guajiros would result in casualties. The colonel could not hope to be so fortunate to win not only a victory, but a victory without lost soldiers.

The economic loss alone would make a war against the Guajiros a matter of greater or lesser defeats.

Last night, the syndicate lost millions. But a war might cost more millions.

And what of the political response? When a never-identified gunman, probably Communist or Guajiro, had murdered Justice Minister Rodrigo Lara Bonilla, all of Colombia rose against the syndicates. Only the prompt and very discrete payments of millions of dollars in gold to Swiss accounts of politicians, prosecutors and newsmen bought an eventual return to the climate of live-and-let profit in national politics.

His son demanded war without quarter. But what if bystanders died in a Castro syndicate frontal assault on the Guajiros? What if the Guajiro terror units indiscriminately attacked a town to kill a single Castro officer? What if the colonel's impetuous son initiated an insane war of vendettas, the syndicates and Guajiros striking one another in an out-of-control maelstrom of gang slaughter without strategy or goal other than murder?

While the syndicates fought the Guajiros, the Bolivians would ship thousands of kilograms of cocaine to the north.

"No war, Enrique. Period."

"But we are strong. You have the battalion. You have your own army! Why not use it?"

"I intend to use my forces," the colonel replied guardedly.

"But when? How?"

"I will use my forces," the colonel repeated. "But only in a counterstrike. A surgical application of military force to a target selected by a knowledgeable and calculating commander."

Enrique laughed at him. "Did they teach you to talk like that in the gringo university? Why will you not use your army? All the other syndicates have armies; they will fight. Together, the syndicates can destroy the Guajiros."

The colonel shook his head. "No, my son. I am a commander. I know my business. I will strike when I see my target."

LYONS WALKED POINT through an unending riot of life and color and sound. His boots were silent on the grasses and wet leaves of the trails, and his approach did not alarm the wildlife. Songbirds continued their calls until the silent, shadow-clad stranger passed within reach of them. With a squawk and a flapping of wings colored with pastels, the birds disappeared into the luxuriant growth of the forest. Toucans watched Lyons pass, their staring white eyes like marbles set into the red-and-yellow cowls of their heads.

Following the topographic map captured from the gang soldiers, Lyons led the line of Americans higher into the foothills. The map indicated the positions of plantations and roads, which Lyons avoided. He maintained an even pace for the group, jogging far ahead of the others to study terrain features, then waiting until they approached before continuing.

Sweat soaked his black fatigues, but he ignored the heat and humidity, pausing only to tie on a black weapon-cleaning cloth as a headband to keep the streams of his sweat out of his eyes.

The jungle heat slowed the others. A few times, when the group approached, he heard Davis or Chan-

dler gasping with the exertion. Lyons buzzed Blancanales with his hand radio.

"Salt-tablet time."

"Already administered," the ex-Green Beret
medic answered.

As the morning became afternoon, the heat finally
slowed Lyons. His shoulders ached from carrying the
weight of his heavy Konzak assault shotgun. The
sweat-soaked straps of his pack cut into his chest.
Sweat flowed from under his pack and down his legs.
He continued walking until he came to a tiny stream
running down a lush hillside. Walking uphill sixty
feet through screens of ferns and branches and hanging vines, he found a flat patch of grass. He buzzed
the others.

"When you come to the stream, leave the trail. Cut
uphill. Don't make any tracks. We'll break until it
cools down."

"Three heat casualties and one medic coming,"
Blancanales replied.

Lyons dropped his pack. He tore a branch off a
tree and returned to the trail. As the others staggered
uphill, he brushed out their tracks on the trail. Before
following them, he listened. A fold of hill between
the clearing and the trail blocked their voices and
equipment noise. Then he continued uphill, brushing
out their tracks, rearranging crushed grass and ferns,
before joining the group.

Still in their packs, Davis and Chandler had collapsed on the ground. Gadgets reclined against a tree,
his bare feet in the stream. A few steps uphill, Blancanales filled a plastic bag with the stream's water.

He hung the bag on a sapling and dropped in purification tablets.

Unfolding the map, Lyons motioned Blancanales over to him. "Here's where I think we are. Here's the town where Chandler says the dope boss has got his battalion. There's a road here—" he traced a line across the whorls and curves of the topographic map, then flipping the sheet over, he showed Blancanales the road on the standard map "—that goes to the town. We'll get to the road before dark. Maybe we can take the road straight in during the night."

"Or capture some transportation."

"You've been monitoring that radio?"

"At first. I got an officer who asked for their report. That was on the hour. By the next hour, we'd walked behind a mountain. Nothing since then."

After studying the map, comparing their path to the hills, Lyons pointed to a wide, flat valley. "Give you odds that the patrol was based out of a plantation right there. That's the best land, and it's a straight line from where we hit them. And there's the mountain that blocked their signal."

Nodding, Blancanales checked the map. "When we reach that road, we'll be receiving transmissions from the garrison."

"Wizard!" Lyons got his partner's attention by flicking a stick across the clearing.

"What?"

"Come over here and talk tech."

"My tech's here. You come and talk to me."

Lyons and Blancanales went to him. "Can you put a scanner on the military frequencies?"

Gadgets didn't open his eyes. "Why you think I'm here? Why am I carrying all that heavy gear in my pack? Any more questions?"

"Then put it together now. We'll be out of the radio shadow as soon as we leave here."

"Hey, Ironman! Political!" Chandler called. He motioned the men over to him.

Chandler held a branch thick with small oval leaves. He chewed a handful of leaves, then spat them out. "You know what this is? It's coca."

"What?" Lyons took a handful of the leaves. "Thought it only grew at high altitudes."

"That's what it says in the books. Chew it. You'll feel your mouth go numb."

"Bitter . . ." Lyons said as he handed some leaves to Blancanales.

"That's because it's an alkaloid," Chandler added. "I saw this stuff from time to time along the trail. Thought it had to be something else. But it's coca."

"Dope everywhere," Lyons said as he spat out a green wad. "We've come to the right place."

"This might explain why the various agencies can't link Route Five to the Bolivian and Peruvian coca producers," Chandler went on, excitement creeping into his voice. "Maybe Route Five developed a heat resistant variety of coca. If the gang's growing its own coca and distributing its cocaine through its own pushers, that explains why we can't slip agents into the syndicate."

"Self-contained," Blancanales summarized.

"That's the problem. How do you break through their defenses to get at the leadership?"

Lyons glanced around at the others. "Here we are."

THE GLARE of the afternoon sun flashed off the commuter plane's wings as it banked into a landing approach. Colonel Castro waited at the edge of the runway in a Mercedes. Alone. None of his men or officers would see the North American he welcomed. The colonel had himself driven one of his tinted-window Mercedes to the airstrip. The soldiers and officers of his battalion would not even know who had met the passenger of the plane. Other North Americans would fly to the battalion base later in the afternoon and the next morning. The colonel's aide would welcome those men. But this visitor would speak only with Colonel Castro.

The plane taxied to a stop, but the pilot did not shut off the engine. Colonel Castro accelerated across the asphalt. As a blond-haired North American in a tropical suit stepped from the plane, the colonel leaned across the front seat and threw open the passenger door.

Don Edwards, director of the United States Drug Enforcement Agency office in Bogotá, got into the Mercedes. He shook hands with the colonel.

"I can only stay a few minutes," Edwards told him.

"That will be enough. I have this material ready for you." The colonel passed a folder to the DEA director. "It shows what happened last night and gives whatever information we have learned. It lists the weapons used, the number of men, photographs and measurements of the aircraft's tires. Also, a chemical analysis of the cocaine stolen.''

Edwards looked up from the folder. ''Ten million dollars' worth?''

''I suffered an equal loss in buildings and equipment.''

''If we get a line on them, you want us to grab these people?''

''No. I require only the identification of the gang involved.''

''Guajiros, huh? We've got plenty of informers in their gangs. We should be able to get the information.''

''Then we will eliminate the gang.''

''That won't necessarily get your cocaine back.''

''That is not my objective.''

''Ten million dollars' worth? You're letting it go?''

''It is more important that I eliminate the gang that has challenged me. If I do not, they will return. I could lose ten million a day in the raids.''

''Tell you what. We get the chance, we'll bust them and grab the stuff. Pay me ten percent. You'll get the gang and the shit.''

''No. I want no link between your agency and this operation. Absolutely no link.''

''Ten million dollars. Maybe fifty million, street price.''

''I considered that.''

''So it's a write-off?''

"My priority is to restore discipline."

"All right," Edwards said as he flipped through the folder. "Very professional.... I have some information that may impact on this. There is a special antiterrorist unit somewhere in Colombia. One of our pilots in California requested a plane for a shuttle flight. No stated destination. The plane landed in Medellín last night—"

"Medellín? What time?"

"Approximately two in the morning. Why?"

The colonel shrugged. "Continue."

"When I got the message about the attack out at El Cristal, at first I thought it might have been them."

"Americans attacking El Cristal?"

"They've done it in other places. Mounted full military assaults on positions, using aircraft and heavy weapons."

"How many men are in this terror unit?"

"Three. However, they hire mercenaries or join local gangs when they need them."

"Are you suggesting they could have—"

"No, Colonel. Someone stole a helicopter from a Ministry of the Interior hangar at the airport about three-thirty. I am sure it was this unit. They left the agency jet and took the helicopter. Here are the descriptions of the three men and here's a photograph of our pilot."

Colonel Castro knew that a DEA plane had landed twenty minutes before the arrival of his son. The presence of the special unit could not be dismissed as a coincidence.

"How could it possibly affect my business?"

"I don't know, Colonel. But you watch out, okay?"

Edwards left the Mercedes. A minute later the plane lifted off, returning Director Edwards to Bogotá.

12

From a hillside overlooking the road to Colina Blanca, Gadgets Schwarz monitored the battalion radio frequencies. He and Blancanales worked together, Gadgets scanning the frequencies and recording the transmissions, Blancanales reviewing the cassette tapes and taking notes. Davis, out of condition and exhausted by the day's walking, rested with them. He occasionally answered technical points on aircraft or distances. The three men worked in a green semi-darkness, a triple-level canopy of jungle concealing them from airborne observation. Tangled walls of ferns and vines rose all around them.

Lyons and Chandler watched the road. Though the captured map showed two roads—one rising from the vast lowlands to the east, a second crossing the mountains to approach the isolated garrison from the west—they saw only the road coming from the east. Like a copper tape, the red-dirt road cut through a hundred tones of green, beginning somewhere in the afternoon haze, appearing on the sides of hills, disappearing, then curving around the ridgeline where Able Team waited for sunset. From where Lyons and Chandler watched, they could not see more than a few hundred yards of the road past them, but across a valley, they saw Colina Blanca.

Colina Blanca, the White Hill. An accident of geology had formed an upjutting mountain of white limestone. Erosion and landslides kept the steep limestone mountainsides scoured of jungle growth, creating one white hill in a horizon of green. The near-vertical mountainsides also served as natural walls, limiting the approach of any attacking force to only the roads.

Or the air. Through binoculars, Lyons watched aircraft landing at the battalion's airfield. In an hour he had counted three light planes arriving. One plane had left. He considered the number of flights unusual for the isolated garrison headquarters.

"Troop truck," Chandler told him.

Lyons focused the binoculars on the road. An OD truck rattled down the road, clouds of red dust rising behind the wheels. Lyons lost sight of the truck as it passed below them, then, after it rounded the curve, he looked down into the open truck. He saw only four soldiers in the back. The cargo took his attention.

The four soldiers braced a Browning 50-caliber machine gun, which was pedestal mounted and fitted with an unusual oversized sight system. Steel rings had been mounted on off-sets from the line of aim. Lyons had seen a similar sighting arrangement on ComBloc 12.7mm machine guns modified for anti-aircraft fire. He studied the weapon for a moment, then the swirling dust obscured the truck.

"You see that?" he asked Chandler.

"Yeah, a machine gun."

"I mean the sights."

"No, I didn't notice. I'm not up on weapons."

"It's been set up to be an antiaircraft gun." Lyons keyed his hand radio and described the modified machine gun to the others. "What have you heard on their radios?" he asked.

"Hot times, man. General alert."

"They found the helicopter?"

"No. They're not even looking for it. And no noise about the missing boys. Seems they got hit by Gua-heroes. Ask Mr. Prosecutor what a—"

Lyons put the radio to Chandler's ear. "Guajiros? Yeah, I know more than I want to know. Are they here?"

"They some gang?"

"They're an army of gangs. The Colombian gangs hate them. It's like the Italian Mafia against the Harlem syndicates in the U.S. What about them?"

"General alert, man. All that's on the radio is Gua-heroes. They is coming."

Chandler passed the radio back to Lyons. "How will that affect us?"

"Who knows?"

They maintained their watch for another hour. Then, as the sun neared the distant horizon of Andean peaks, they moved down the mountainside. Lyons and Blancanales rushed downslope to the road, Lyons taking a position at one curve, Blancanales at another. They watched for approaching trucks as the other three men thrashed down the mountain.

Crossing the road, they found concealment only one step down the roadway's embankment. Gadgets buzzed his partners.

"No chance—" he coughed as he breathed the fine red dust "—to hitchhike here. Gotta get another position if we're—"

"Pol!" Lyons demanded. "Is it clear?"

"Nothing on the road."

"Move it, Wizard. Get those other two on their feet."

Straining against the weight of their packs, they struggled three hundred yards uphill. Darkness came before they found Lyons. Stumbling over the rocks and ruts, the light failing by the minute, Gadgets finally called out, "Ironman? Where you hiding?"

A voice answered. "Gua-heroes! Mata-los!"

Gadgets forced a very deliberate laugh. "Not funny!"

The tiny point of a penlight revealed Lyons's position. Stepping into the brush, Gadgets pushed aside a branch. Powder-fine dust spilled over him. He choked and coughed, spitting dust.

His hand radio buzzed three times and he dropped flat. Looking up, he saw Chandler and Davis silhouetted against the gray sky. "Down, cherries! That's an alarm. Don't you ever learn?"

Beside them, Lyons whispered into his radio, "What's coming?"

"Transportation," Blancanales replied. "There's a truck a few miles downhill. We want to ride in, or walk?"

"You want to chance it?"

"Walking on the road will be a risk."

Lyons whispered to Gadgets, "Want a truck?"

"No, I want an air-conditioned motor home with a

shower and a water bed. And three starlets. And a—"

Ignoring the answer, Lyons spoke into the radio again. "How can we stop it?"

"Nine millimeter through the sidewall of a tire. They'll stop to change the tire and we take them."

"Those underpowered nines won't puncture a tire. I've tried."

"I'll use a full-powered nine millimeter. If I fire it through the Beretta, the suppressor will hide the flash and the blowout will cover whatever noise there is."

Lyons considered the improvised solution. The Beretta 93-R autopistols Gadgets and Blancanales carried had been modified for silence with suppressors and underpowered cartridges. A full-powered FMJ slug would puncture a truck's tire, but the use of a full-powered cartridge required field-stripping the pistol and changing the mainspring.

"Can you change the spring before—"

"Ninety-five seconds, blindfolded," the Politician shot back.

"Do it. But we won't make the move until after they change the tire."

They waited in the dark. Insects found them; mosquitoes and gnats buzzed around them. Davis jumped when something found his swollen ant stings. He slapped at it and knocked it off, then Chandler muttered and threw the insect farther away. Gadgets jumped. Thrashing about in the darkness, Gadgets killed the thing with slaps.

"Quit the three stooges routine!" Lyons spat out, exasperated.

"That was a giant centipede!" Gadgets whispered. "Or a snake with a hundred legs."

"The truck!"

A rattling sound approached. Low-gearing up the grade, equipment and fenders banging on every rock and pothole, a truck appeared several hundred yards down the mountain. Headlights flashed around a curve, then the truck passed behind trees.

A tire blew out.

Lurching, the tire flapping on the rim, the truck reappeared. Lyons pressed his face to the dusty matting of leaves as the truck's brakes squealed. Doors opened. Two men called back and forth, cursing in Spanish. The headlights went out. Blinkers flashed red. Lyons looked up. Fifty yards away, he saw a flashlight bobbing and weaving as a man took tools out of a box. Another man set a cassette player on the truck's flatbed. Disco rhythms blasted the darkness.

The two men worked on the truck in the glow of the flashlight. Bracing a hydraulic jack under the frame, the men took turns levering the handle.

Lyons leaned against Gadgets, using his body to block the sound of his whispering into this hand radio. "Political. You holding your position?"

"Watching the road."

"I'm moving into pistol range."

"Go."

Returning his radio to its carrying case on his web gear, Lyons whispered to Gadgets, "You heard?"

"Forget creeping up on them. There's snakes and things out there. I'll use my Interdynamic kit, pop them from here."

"I don't trust those little .22s."

"Macho, macho."

As Lyons shrugged out of his gear, Gadgets converted his Colt Automatic Rifle to the silent mode. He dropped the 30-round magazine out of the CAR, snapped in one of the replacement mags of twenty Interdynamic 5.56mm cartridges. The Interdynamic cartridges contained reduced powder charges that propelled 185-grain slugs at the subsonic velocity of 890 feet per second. The silencer slipped down over the flash-suppressor and locked. The reduced charges of the cartridges did not generate the chamber pressure to cycle the bolt, therefore totally eliminating all mechanical noise. Together, the Interdynamic cartridges and the Maxim multibaffle silencer converted the CAR to a silenced rifle with deadly accuracy to two hundred yards. Gadgets pressed the base of the magazine to check its seating.

"Ready to go," he whispered to Lyons.

"Then I'm on my way." With his black weapon-cleaning cloth tied over his face, Lyons crawled through the powderlike dust at the side of the road. He moved slowly, not wanting to raise the superfine dust, pushing aside fronds and stalks, feeling insects skittering across his hands. Mosquitoes buzzed around his head but did not bite, perhaps repelled by the chemical odors of the solvents and oils in the black cloth on his face.

In the thigh pockets of his fatigue pants, Lyons carried only his hand radio and his silenced Colt Government Model. Redesigned and hand-machined by Andrzej Konzaki to incorporate the innovations of Beretta technology, the interior mechanisms of the Colt no longer resembled what Browning had invented and patented. Like the Beretta 93-R pistols Blancanales and Gadgets carried, the Colt featured a fold-down lever and oversized trigger guard to provide a positive two-hand grip. But it fired silenced, full-powered .45-caliber slugs, in semiauto and 3-shot-burst modes.

Lyons stayed below the shoulder of the road. Above him, the flashing blinkers projected red light onto the dust-heavy overhanging branches. He continued along below the road until he heard the disco music and clanking tools immediately above him. Infinitely slowly, he eased his head above the embankment.

A few steps away, the two syndicate soldiers rolled a tire into position, then kicked it onto the hub. The men had stripped off their shirts, their sweaty torsos gleaming in the weak light. Lyons watched the men he would kill. Though he could not understand their quick and idiomatic Spanish, he studied their tattoos and scars. One man had patterns of obscene illustrations and gang symbols worked into his back and arms. Knife scars defaced the other man's multicolored tattoos of spiders and the Virgin Mary.

They tightened the lugnuts. Lyons eased back the slide of his silenced Colt to chamber the first 185-grain hollowpoint. He waited until they finished with the last lugnut and returned the tools to the box.

Then he shot them, the first man dying instantly as a hollowpoint exploded through the base of his brain, the second man taking a hollowpoint through the heart.

"Move it, Political!" Lyons said into his hand radio. Then he shouted out to the others, "Bring my gear."

Checking the pockets of both corpses, he found a hypodermic kit and a pack of pornographic playing cards in the Virgin Mary's pockets, and a wallet with photos of children in the other man's pockets. He dumped the corpses off the road. In the cab of the truck he found the keys in the ignition. A radio and two FN FAL folding-stock pararifles and ammunition bandoliers lay on the seat. He left the radio for Gadgets and put the rifles in the back.

"Davis! Chandler! You're riding cargo class with me."

"Here's your pack," Chandler said, passing his gear to him. "And this supershotgun."

"Political! You're driving! Put on one of their shirts. We might run into a checkpoint."

"Will do."

Seconds later the truck lurched into motion. In the back of the truck, the three men choked in the billowing dust. Lyons passed Chandler the dead soldier's wallet.

"Read through that. See if there's any information we can use."

Chandler flicked on his penlight. For a long moment he looked at the snapshots of the dead man posing with his wife and children, then up at the silhouette of Lyons. Lyons saw the glance.

"What?"

"This reminds me of when I was a lieutenant, going through my casualties' personal things. Sorting everything out to send back to their families."

"Wrong memory, Prosecutor. Those are the personal effects of a dead enemy."

"Tell it to his children. I think that—"

"Don't think. You'll learn not to think if you want to stay sane and alive. I got enough dead people to think about at night. Good men, good women. Not gang soldiers. With luck, no one will ever tell his children that their father was a dope soldier. So stifle the memories and read the cards."

Headlights appeared behind them. Lyons slapped the cab and shouted, "Accelerate. We got traffic behind us."

Blancanales increased his speed. But the headlights gained. Sideslipping, cutting the curves so close that their stake sides smashed through branches, the trucks closed the distance.

"What's their rush?" Davis asked.

Above the headlights, a muzzle flashed. Heavy-caliber slugs tore past Lyons. "They're shooting! Speed it up!"

Davis grabbed a grenade from his captured web gear. Not stopping to check the type or effect, he jerked out the pin and threw.

A bang sprayed metallic fire over the road and the bush. Branches burst into flame. The burning chemicals and wood illuminated gray smoke swirling from the points of white phosphorus. The lead truck drove through the smoke and flames without slowing.

As their stolen truck swept through a long curve, Lyons looked back and saw three trucks behind them. The white light and flames illuminated the road. As the second truck drove through the fires, he saw who rode in the back of the stake-sided truck.

Men in a miss-matched assortment of uniforms. Wearing cowboy hats and motorcycle helmets. Armed with Kalashnikovs and rocket-propelled grenade launchers.

"Guajiros!"

13

A rocket screamed over the truck. Blast shock slammed them, bits of rock spraying the truck, shredded wood and green pulp coming an instant later. Davis dropped down flat on the boards as high-velocity rifle slugs ripped past his head. Slugs hammered the truck, sheet metal clanging and buckling, side slats splintering.

Lyons found the FN pararifles and ammunition he had taken from the dead soldiers. He shoved one rifle and a bandolier into Chandler's hands.

"Forget your M-16. Use this. Aim between the headlights, try to put the bullets into the engine."

Folding out the other rifle's steel stock, Lyons snappointed the rifle at the headlights of the pursuing truck and squeezed the trigger. Nothing. No round in the chamber. Jerking back the cocking handle to load a cartridge, he looked for a target. A hillside protected the Guajiro trucks.

Chandler struggled with his rifle's stock. Lyons leaned over to him and pressed the lock button. The stock swung out. Brass rained down on them as Davis sprayed wild, full-auto fire from his Uzi. Lyons jerked back the FN's cocking actuator for Chandler.

"Thanks, I got it now. There's the truck!"

Headlights came around a turn. This time, Lyons

tried to aim. But Fabrique Nationale did not manufacture nightsights for their standard infantry rifles. The rifles had only the standard-issue fixed-range peep sight. In the darkness, the rifles became almost impossible to aim with any degree of accuracy. Lyons pointed the rifle and fired three shots.

Another rocket launcher flashed. The rocket shrieked over the truck, continuing into the night. The warhead's charge self-destructed in a spray of incandescent metal that rained down on the jungled valley below. Sighting as best he could, Lyons fired shot after shot at the headlights behind them. He did not know if he scored hits. Davis fired long bursts.

"How are you aiming?" Chandler shouted out over the rattling of the truck.

"You can't. These rifles weren't designed for night combat."

"That's great! What do we do?"

"Write the manufacturer! Put out rounds," Lyons yelled as he threw a second bandolier of 7.62mm NATO cartridges to Chandler. Then, leaning over the tailgate, he jammed the muzzle of the pararifle through the lenses of the taillights, breaking the bulbs. He left the pararifle hanging on the side slats. Returning to his gear, Lyons slipped the sling of his Konzak assault shotgun over his head.

Andrzej Konzaki, ex-Marine and master weaponsmith, had fought in the 1st Corps of Vietnam. Unlike the European designers employed by Fabrique Nationale, the ex-Marine knew the value of a weapon that could be employed in the night. The selective-fire 12-gauge shotgun he had designed and handcrafted featured tritium dashes on the back sights and a dot on the fore sight. The assault shotgun could be aimed in total darkness. Lyons lined up the glowing points on the headlights and thumbed the safety–fire-selector down to semiauto.

Whipping through the snaking curves, the first truck gained the protection of a hillside. Lyons sighted on the second truck, holding his aim above and ahead of his target to compensate for the extreme distance and speed, and fired once. He put his tritium sights on line with the third truck and triggered another blast.

Though the number-two and double-ought steel shot would not kill at the extreme range, the steel balls would wound and distract the Guajiros. A distraction might throw off the aim of a man with a rocket launcher.

Chandler and Davis continued firing wild. The road straightened for a few hundred yards. Lyons shouted to Blancanales, "Stop at the curve! We'll hit them on this stretch." Lyons turned to Chandler and Davis. "You two! Reload! Be ready to aim at the lights and fire out a magazine."

Blancanales slowed the truck as he came to the curve. Behind them they had a direct line of fire. Lyons set the Konzak's safety and unhooked the second FN. He took another magazine from Chandler.

The cab's passenger-side door opened and slammed. Gadgets ran around to the tailgate. He clutched Blancanales's M-16/M-203 over-and-under rifle-grenade launcher in his hands. When he reached up to climb over the tailgate, Lyons shoved him down.

"Get back up front! Pol can't drive and handle the radios, too."

"There's nothing on the radio!"

"This isn't—"

"The truck!"

The Uzi and FN rifles fired in one long burst. Gadgets scrambled up the tailgate as brass casings fell on him. He turned to aim the hybrid rifle-grenade launcher, but the others had scored on the truck.

A headlight went black, while the other weaved across the narrow road, the truck careening into the mountainside, then curving for the drop-off. In the headlights of the convoy, they saw men abandoning the driverless truck. One form raised a weapon and its muzzle flashed. Two men ran from the crowd with a tripod-mounted machine gun.

As slugs zipped past the truck, Gadgets sighted the M-16/M-203 and fired. A 40mm grenade arched across the hundreds of yards of distance. Though the high explosive popped short, silhouettes scattered. The two men with the machine gun dragged their weapon to cover.

"Move it, get us out of here!" Lyons screamed as he jammed another magazine into the FN and sighted on the second truck. Aiming directly into the headlights, he managed to get a sight-picture despite the darkness. He fired a long burst, struggling against the recoil to hold the rifle on line, then Blancanales took the truck around the corner.

Far behind them they heard the smashing sounds of a truck crashing down the mountainside.

"One down!" Davis cheered.

"Maybe two!" Chandler added.

The road curved around a projecting ridgeline.

Standing in the back, they had a momentary panorama of the mountains and valley. Ahead, they saw the lights of buildings. Behind, they saw two sets of headlights illuminating clouds of dust. Farther back on the road, they saw more headlights appearing and disappearing in the trees. A line of five trucks raced up the mountain road.

"There it is, cherries!" Gadgets shouted out. "Waste one, there's always more."

"We don't know they are Guajiros," Chandler countered.

Lyons laughed. "Mr. Prosecutor, what's the difference? Everyone up here wants to kill you."

Gadgets pointed ahead. "Roadblock!"

Parked trucks guarded the entrance to the town of Colina Blanca. On both sides of the road soldiers stood ready with rifles and submachine guns. Lyons leaned over the side slats and shouted into the driver's window.

"Get past them, Pol. If they don't check us, once we're inside, we got a chance—"

Slugs hammered the truck, punching through metal, a tire exploding, ricochets whining into the distance. As the truck bumped along on the flapping tire, Lyons looked back and saw the Guajiro trucks closing on them.

Riflemen stood shoulder-to-shoulder above the cab of the leading truck, their rifles a horizontal band of flashes as they fired full-auto.

Blancanales leaned out the window and shouted in Spanish to the soldiers manning the roadblock. "Guajiros! Guajiros! They're coming behind us!"

"Down!" Lyons told the men around him. "Down, don't let them see us as we go through."

A rocket launcher flashed. For an incredible instant, as the rocket streaked toward them, Lyons thought he saw the tip of the warhead rushing at his nose. But the rocket hit short, exploding twenty yards behind the truck.

Flame and a vast ball of dust enveloped the back of the truck. Blancanales shouted a command to the men at the roadblock in Spanish, and the weapons of the soldiers fired in one roaring fusillade of full-auto, hundreds of bullets tearing past the bumping, clattering truck.

The cab of the pursuing Guajiro truck disintegrated as the combined fire of rifles and submachine guns hit. Tempered glass sparkled in the air, the headlights died, the driver died, tracer ricochets pinwheeled into the night. Forms fell from the sides of the truck.

As the soldiers continued firing, Blancanales drove through the roadblock without slowing. An officer ran after the truck, but Blancanales left the roadblock and firefight behind as he whipped the truck through a shuddering left-hand turn and hurtled through the narrow main street of the town.

Old stone and stucco buildings lined the cobblestone lane. Streetlights illuminated the corners, thousands of insects orbiting the bulbs. Few of the shops and homes showed lights. As the truck bumped past, shopkeepers slammed their shutters. A woman hurried from one door to another. Everyone in town could hear the fighting.

Blancanales saw a wide side street. Forcing the

truck through another turn, he drove through a plaza lined by boarded-up market stalls and shops. A woman shut the door of a café. Dogs retreated to the shadows. A stark white church stood at one end.

Lyons leaned forward. "Look for a place," he said.

Blancanales shouted back, "To hide this wreck? What do you think I'm doing?"

"Then do it."

Engine noise came from the sky, and Lyons looked up to see the town's lights reflected from the underside of a plane. A barrel fell from the plane's open passenger door, and a man leaned out the door to watch the impact.

The barrel hit the ground a few streets away. Lyons heard a flat bang, then streamers of flame arched in all directions as the improvised napalm canister scattered burning gel on roofs. The plane circled. Orange light from the petrochemical fires lit the underside of the plane.

Throughout the area of the town and garrison, soldiers aimed their rifles at the bomber. The plane dropped another incendiary barrel. Fire lit the night somewhere past the town. The plane circled back.

At the entrance to the town, the firefight continued. Rifles cracked in ripping bursts. Machine guns boomed over the smaller weapons. The explosion of an RPG brought a stunned instant of quiet from the defending Castro syndicate soldiers, then the firing resumed.

"Looks like we got a distraction," Lyons commented to the others.

"Maybe more than that," Chandler added. "Those Guajiros might overrun the other gang."

"Hope those scum annihilate each other." Lyons leaned forward again and said to Blancanales, "Try to get through the gates of the base."

"Which way?"

"I don't know! You're driving—"

Flame exploded on a narrow lane. A gob of burning gel splattered the back of the truck. Davis tried to stomp it out and his boot burned. Stomping, hot-footing in the back of the truck, scraping the boot against the slat boards, he finally got the fire off his boot. They let the spot of gel burn.

Blancanales guided the truck through the streets. The shot-out tire flapped, and the truck lurched along on the cobblestones. Gadgets looked ahead and saw soldiers standing in front of a café. With rifles in their hands, they watched the sky for the bombing plane.

"Down! Doper goons!"

The North Americans went flat. The group of soldiers watched the truck pass.

The plane overhead dropped more barrels. Flames rose from the town and the garrison. Ahead, Able Team saw the lighted perimeter of the army facility. The Guajiro plane circled the base, bombing, using the lights of the perimeter, the barracks, and the airfield for targets.

Another plane appeared in the sky. A streak of flame shot from the side and a line of tracers raked the base.

The perimeter lights went out. One by one, lights

everywhere on the base went dark as the soldiers finally reacted to the air assault.

Blancanales approached a gate, and the sentries waved flashlights to hurry the truck through. Despite the flapping tire, Blancanales accelerated, bumping through the gate just as a line of jeeps and trucks sped out, racing to the continuing firefight on the road.

White light came from the sky. Lyons looked up, squinting into the glare of a magnesium flare descending on a miniature parachute. The planes continued their bombing and strafing of the base.

The bomber plane circled a target. In the white glare of the descending flare, Lyons saw a man in the cabin doorway. The light gleamed off a canister at his feet.

A green light streaked upward from a rooftop, and Lyons heard the hammering of a squad automatic weapon. The unseen machine gunner held his aim on the low-flying plane, the heavy-caliber slugs raking the wings and fuselage. Then a tracer hit the canister in the door.

The plane instantly became a flying ball of fire, losing altitude, spinning as it fell. The wing tanks flashed an instant before impact. An entire block of garrison buildings disappeared in flames.

Flat on his face in the back of the truck, Chandler laughed. "All right! We're in! Enrique Raul Castro, here we come. We've come to get you!"

Gadgets looked out at the soldiers running everywhere in the darkness and flames. "Yeah, and just exactly which one of you is Mr. Castro?"

14

In the chaos of the attack—hundreds of weapons firing, conflicting radio reports, panicked soldiers shouting—Colonel Castro organized a coherent defense to the combined air and truck assault.

First, he dispatched on-duty guard units to reinforce the platoon fighting at the entrance to the town. He knew the Guajiro invaders must be stopped on the road or his soldiers would be fighting door-to-door throughout Colina Blanca.

Then he ordered his aides to black out the base and the town. Even the perimeter lights had to be switched off until he managed to destroy the planes bombing and strafing the battalion positions.

The colonel directed the defense from the balcony of his office. His aides remained in the shelter of the mansion's limestone walls, relaying radio and telephone reports by shouting out to him. Cocking his pistol, the colonel rushed into the office.

"All of you! You with the telephone, outside! You with the field radio, outside! Outside!"

The aides took their equipment and maps outside. A magnesium flare popped high above the base. Descending on a tiny parachute, the searing point of white light illuminated the entire mountaintop. Above, the bomber circled for another strike.

Colonel Castro aimed his pistol at the plane and fired careful shots. Following their commander's lead, the others on the balcony fired their pistols and submachine guns.

A line of tracers from the base found the bomber. The anonymous machine gunner kept his aim on the moving plane until the fuselage exploded in a ball of fire. Rolling as it fell, the flaming plane exploded again as the gasoline in the wing tanks ignited.

The crash drove the plane through the roof and into the interior of a barracks building. Wreckage and flames spread over the rooftop. Seconds later, shots came from the second-story windows.

The aides and soldiers on the balcony cheered. The colonel screamed to make himself heard. "Shut up! That is not a victory! You see the base? It's burning. Any more victories like that one and we will be defeated!"

The machine gunner sent another line of green tracers up at the second plane. Veering, the Guajiro pilot took the plane to an altitude of three thousand feet. The autofire from the side door resumed, and orange tracers scratched a line from the flashing muzzle to the base. The machine gunner on the ground tried to maintain his aim on the plane, but gravity defeated his fire and the green tracers from his weapon dropped back, burned out, without scoring.

"Lieutenant Rivas!" the colonel called over a young officer who talked on a telephone. "Contact the airfield. I want two machine gun teams to report to the field and stand by. When the machine guns are in place and ready, then an armed helicopter is to attempt to down that aircraft. The helicopter is not to attempt to lift off until it has protection from the machine guns. If the plane breaks off and retreats, the helicopter is not to pursue. A plane with radar is to stand by. If the Guajiro plane returns to base, our plane is to follow it and attempt to get a location."

With a salute the lieutenant relayed the instructions. The colonel found a radio operator. "Get on the general frequency. Announce the attack. Declare an extreme alert. I want every facility ready for combat. I want a report from every facility. This attack is probably a diversion. The processing centers must be ready to repel a raid."

"And you," he said as he pointed at another radio operator, "I want you to scan the frequencies. Find the frequency of the Guajiros. Do not stop. Scan the frequencies all night if you have to."

Colonel Castro gave other officers other responsibilities. "You, Lopez! Assemble an assault squad. The best soldiers you have. Take them down to the airfield and wait. Tell them to take all the ammunition and grenades they can carry. You, Garcia! Find a radio and maintain contact with the guards on the roads. The Guajiros might come on the western road also. Tell the guards to stop all trucks. None of our forces are to move by truck. There is too much risk of ambush."

An orderly ran to him. "Colonel, Sergeant Munoz is falling back from the roadblock. He has received heavy casualties and he needs—"

"Tell him I will shoot him if he abandons his position!'' the colonel shouted. ''Radio him. Tell him to spread out his soldiers on the mountainsides. He must stop the Guajiros.''

''But Colonel, Sergeant—''

''But nothing! If he retreats, he will be shot! Tell him that!''

A lone North American sat on the tiles near the balcony's edge. Bracing a NATO-caliber Galil autorifle on the stone railing, he fired single shots at the strafing plane high overhead. As the leader of a special enforcement unit based in Bogotá, Larry Fields maintained his cold, arrogant demeanor despite the confusion of the officers and soldiers around him.

Colonel Castro had summoned Fields to the battalion base to brief him on the raid and to organize an investigation. Now the colonel decided to employ Fields directly against the Guajiros.

''Mr. Fields! Do not waste your time and bullets!''

''Got to get into it. Can't just stand here and watch the show.''

''I have another task for you. Take that orderly and a radio. Find some men who aren't hiding and crying and reinforce Sergeant Munoz at the eastern side of the town.''

''Sure, Colonel. Sounds like a good time.''

Fields picked up his bandolier of Galil magazines and rushed downstairs. The colonel resumed his pacing and shouting. He issued orders as he watched the fires spreading in the town and the garrison. Then a thought stopped him in midstride. My son! Where is my son?

IN THE GAME LOUNGE of the mansion's basement, protected from the fighting by yards of limestone, Enrique Raul Castro tried to enflame his courage with cocaine. A pornographic film played on a video-cassette recorder, images of red-lipped women with lithe white bodies flashing on the projection screen, intercut with scenes of one woman contorting to perform cinematic intercourse with five men simultaneously, using her body and both hands.

A hundred grams of pure cocaine lay on a hand mirror. Enrique did not bother to divide the cocaine into lines. He put a plastic straw to his nostril and jammed the other end into glittering cocaine. Clamping off the other nostril with a finger, he snorted hard, the suction of his lungs pulling the powder across his nasal membranes and deep into his lungs. He exhaled, switched nostrils, then sucked down another dose of powder.

Closing his eyes, he drifted. His nose and throat chilled. His mind chilled, his fear and panic diminishing. Outside, the hammering of rifles and machine guns continued. But in his mind, his pulse pounded, every beat sending blood roaring through his arteries. He flexed his arm, felt the sinews and muscles tighten.

Like steel.

He plunged the straw into the cocaine again, pulled down two more deep snorts.

Steel! Floating in silence and darkness, his body and mind gleamed like polished steel. Now he would face the attack. He opened his eyes and saw a white-blond girl—a Dane, a Swede?—servicing a long line of men. Enrique had not seen this performance before. Transfixed by the scene, studying the flicking of her tongue in the camera's extreme close-ups, he watched her finish one man and immediately go on to the next. Semen and sweat ran down her face. She seemed determined to achieve a record in a speed and number competition.

Fascinating. Enrapturing. Enrique wondered how he could meet someone like that talented young woman. Perhaps during his next business trip to Europe. He could delegate his father's business to aides while he cruised the brothels. Someone knocking at the door interrupted his fantasies.

"Who is it?"

"Luis...."

Enrique staggered to the door. He had to reach for the knob twice before he grasped it. Finally he succeeded in turning the knob and opening the door.

Luis Ortega wore the uniform of a Colombian army lieutenant. In the syndicate organization, he served as a clerk in the transport office. His responsibilities included the scheduling and routing of cocaine shipments to the north.

By chance, months before, Enrique had cursed his father loudly and criticized his conservative production and marketing of cocaine. Ortega had heard Enrique. Alcohol and cocaine made Enrique brave and loquacious. Sharing a bottle of Chivas Regal with Ortega, Enrique talked for hours, blasting his father's rule and bragging of the world-spanning drug syndicate he would create when he took control of his father's enterprise. Ortega had listened and encouraged Enrique to make plans. In the following months, they became close friends and conspirators, Enrique the talker, Ortega the listener.

"Doesn't the colonel want you in the battle?"

Enrique spat cocaine on the carpet. "He has soldiers. He has his army. I would be only one more soldier. Has he destroyed the Guajiros yet?"

The lieutenant shook his head. "It is very serious. This might be the last night of the Castro empire."

"What! But he has the battalion, the militiamen, the planes and helicopters—"

"The Guajiros attack from the roads and from the air. The base is in flames. The Guajiros infiltrated assault forces and they are fighting at the checkpoints into the village. The colonel is so desperate that he has ordered that men who retreat will be shot. He has told his most loyal pilots to stand by at their planes in case he loses the mountain."

Enrique shuddered. While he sat here staring at video girls he could not touch, he could have been left behind during the evacuation, he could have been left to the mercy of the Guajiros, who skinned men alive and poured gasoline on the raw, bleeding, screaming....

Despite the danger, he must go and stand at his father's side. Only then could he be sure he would get a seat on a flight out of the defeat. Panicked, he lurched for the door. Luis stopped him with an offer.

"Now is the time to negotiate...."

"How? With the Guajiros? They are animals!"

Luis smiled. "Not animals. Competitors. Fellow Colombians. Denied their rightful place in the society. Forced by the policies of men like your father to fight for a place in the business. Do you think they would not rather enjoy peaceful cooperation between the syndicates? The market for drugs is without limits. North America wants more than we can produce. Europe wants an equal and equally impossible supply. We could all be rich. In truth, it is class antagonism. The elitists of our nation will not recognize the hopes of the lower classes, therefore the lower classes must fight for their rightful share. Listen, outside they fight. They will win, if not tonight, then tomorrow or the next day. This is your opportunity!''

"How? How is it an opportunity?"

"If you negotiate a resolution to this problem, which is actually only a business problem, then not only will there be peace, but you can oust those who live in the past. Your father would send all his soldiers to death to preserve his inherited colonial privileges. Are you willing to use your intelligence? Instead of wasting the lives of soldiers? Instead of wasting your wealth on war when there is enough wealth for everyone? The decision is yours. Give me the word."

"Do you have contact with them?"

"Not now. But I could—"

Just then, soldiers looked in the door. One called out, "Lieutenant Castro! Your father looks for you!"

Enrique stuck out his chest. He commanded, "You! Soldier. Come here." Going to a closet, he pulled out an American M-60 machine gun—loaded, a belt of cartridges dangling—and three OD cans of belted 7.62mm ammunition. He passed the ammunition to the soldier. Slipping the M-60's sling over his shoulder, Enrique started out. He turned back to his friend and co-conspirator and said, "Come. I must rejoin the fight. But stay with me. We have much to discuss."

Following the soldiers, Enrique and Luis climbed the wide stone steps from the ornate basement. Decades before, untrained *indigena* slaves had quarried and carved the stone in patterns taken from photos in books. The *indigenas* had created strangely stylized designs, the geometric Castilian motifs becoming vines and flowers and symbols from the local religions. European faces became expressionistic masks like those seen in *indigena* rites. But of all their translations of the conquerors' art, the *indigenas* gave one series of repeating symbolic faces a new and bizarre appearance: the gargoyles copied from the cathedrals of Europe. The general had often speculated aloud to his guests that the *indigena* artists had taken hallucinogens before beginning their work.

Now, as Enrique passed the surreal faces emerging from the walls, his mind seething with the narcotic intoxication of several grams of pure cocaine, the faces seemed to move and turn, to stare at him as he passed, the stone eyes regarding him. One face bared its fangs.

Enrique startled back, his drug-twisted reason utterly gone for an instant, the M-60 coming up in his hands. The muzzle flashed point-blank into the horror-mask.

Stone chips flew. Cartridge casings rang on the steps. The flash and noise shattered Enrique's cocaine delirium. Seeing the alarmed faces of the soldiers, he laughed off his hallucination.

"An accident! Continue...."

Behind him, Lieutenant Ortega smiled. This dope-crazed degenerate, this playboy son of a syndicate warlord could be manipulated to betray his father.

And that betrayal would make Ortega rich.

15

"So where is little Rique?" Gadgets asked. "That is the question...."

Parked in a vehicle yard, Able Team held a quick conference in the back of the captured truck. No sentries patrolled the rows of parked trucks and construction vehicles, and the North Americans had the yard to themselves. The battle raged while they talked, the Guajiros continuing their attack from the air and the road.

The plane circled high overhead, directing intermittent machine-gun fire down on the base. Without lights, only the silhouette of the wings and fuselage against the stars and the tracers from the machine gun revealed its position. But from the altitude the plane maintained, the gunner could only harass the battalion.

Shooting and explosions from the town indicated that the Guajiros in the trucks presented a more serious threat. The volume of fire rose and fell, the weapons of the attackers and defenders sometimes firing in wild volleys, other times dying down to the firing of individual rifles as soldiers maneuvered for positions.

But none of the action threatened the North Americans. The plane circled over the main section of the base and the white limestone palace set on the highest point of the mountaintop. All the machine-gun fire went into the barracks or the palace or the airfield.

"Where is Enrique the rich boy?" Lyons asked. "Do rich kids fight for daddy's money when there are soldiers to do the dying? Enrique Castro is where it's safest, right there—" Lyons pointed to the limestone palace rising above the sprawling battalion base.

Chandler looked at the mountaintop palace. "Are you suggesting we attack that place? I don't know if—"

"No way," Gadgets interrupted. "Repeat, we will not do that."

"Did I say that?" Lyons demanded. "I said he's in there. I didn't—"

"You've been known to try things like that," Gadgets answered. "But we agreed, right? No more suicide assaults. Right?"

"Right." Lyons did not argue the point. "What I'm saying is that if he's in there, it's unlikely that we can go in and get him."

"Perhaps an infiltration," Blancanales suggested.

"And then get him out?" Davis asked, incredulous. "And back to the helicopter? And then find someplace to refuel? And then get him to the airport and on the plane? I didn't think you specialists made arrests."

"To kill him," Lyons stated. "No one's talking about making an arrest. You want us to arrest him, Mr. Prosecutor? You bring a warrant?"

"What for?" Chandler asked. "The case against him got dismissed. It would just be another circus session. But this time, after they released Castro, they'd put me away for ten thousand years for violation of due process and illegal extradition."

"So there it is," Gadgets concluded. "Death verdict. But the question remains, how do we do little Rique?"

"How do we get him out of there?" Chandler looked up at the palace.

Blancanales considered the question. "The Castros and the battalion's senior officers will stay there throughout the fight. However, if the Guajiros overrun the base, the Castros will evacuate. They have planes and helicopters," Blancanales said as he pointed to the airfield, "and they will use them."

Lyons laughed. "Standard Latin American tactic, unless they lose. Then the rich go to Miami and the soldiers stay to do the dying."

"Jokes won't kill the Castros," Blancanales continued. "If the Guajiros break through the perimeter, the Castros will either go to the airfield to take a plane or get a helicopter to take them out of the palace up there. But if the Guajiros don't—"

"If they don't overrun this place," Lyons interrupted, "then the Castros don't move. And I don't think the Guajiros can do it. One convoy of goon soldiers and one light plane with a machine gun against a battalion? It isn't going to happen."

"Unless maybe we help them!" Gadgets pointed to the airfield. "We could do a number on the fuel storage or the ammo dump. Demoralize this place.

They see the place flaming, they'll run. Guajiros come in, the Castros split. Bang, bang, we do them.''

Blancanales shook his head. "I don't believe that would defeat these soldiers. They're real soldiers and they're putting up a good fight."

"Yeah, infinite ifs," Gadgets admitted. "But have you got a better idea? Or do we sit here and talk and wait?"

"Patience, my ass," Blancanales joked, yielding to his partners' aggression. "Let's go out and kill something."

Transferring their gear and weapons to another transport truck, the North Americans laid down in the back of the truck and concealed themselves with tarps. Blancanales drove the truck from the vehicle yard.

Warehouses separated the vehicle yard from the airstrip. Trucks and skiploaders were parked in the lane between the warehouse and the aircraft hangars. Blancanales saw no soldiers near the warehouses, and only one warehouse office showed lights.

A hundred yards away, through a hangar's side door, Blancanales saw soldiers gathering. Lines of equipment—ammunition cases, automatic weapons on bipods, and what looked like antiarmor rockets in fiberboard tubes—had been laid out on the floor in preparation for a mission.

Blancanales continued past the doorway. He saw a space in a line of trucks and he backed into it. Leaving the truck, he stepped to the cargo bed.

"Wait," he told the others.

Slinging an FN pararifle over his shoulder, he

walked past the side doors of the hangars to the airstrip. Soldiers stood guard everywhere, but they watched the sky and the distant fence. A machine gun crew waited for the Guajiro plane to fly over the hangars. Inside two hangars, mechanics worked on planes, while in the last hangar, the soldiers assembled their equipment near two helicopters.

He saw trucks parked on the airstrip to block the landing of any planes.

But he saw no tanker trucks or above-ground fuel storage tanks in the area of the airstrip or the hangars. He stood in the shadows, watching the activities of the soldiers and technicians for minutes. Then Blancanales returned to his partners.

Standing beside the stake-side transport, he watched the dark lane behind the hangars as he whispered to the others. "No gas trucks. No storage tanks. And it will not be possible for us to move around. Absolutely impossible. There are soldiers and sentries everywhere."

"What about those buildings there?" Lyons pointed. "Those warehouses?"

"No one there."

"Then let's take a look! They've got to keep their gas somewhere." Lyons turned to Chandler. "We're going inside. You and Davis keep watch out here. Stay low, watch. You've got a radio, so if you see anyone coming, give us warning. If they're too close, and you don't want to risk them hearing, give us three clicks. Got it?"

"Good luck in there," Chandler said by way of reply.

"Good luck out here, cherries," Gadgets countered as he snapped left-handed salutes to Chandler and Davis. Then he dropped to the asphalt.

Lyons slung his Konzak over his shoulder and cinched the strap tight. He slipped out his silenced Colt Government Model. He wrapped his black weapon-cleaning rag *ninja*-style around his face and hair, leaving only a slit for his eyes.

Silently the three men of Able Team moved from door to door, trying locks. Gadgets held up his electric lock pick, but Lyons shook his head, pointing to the lighted office a few doors ahead. He held up his Colt Government Model. Gadgets and Blancanales nodded.

Lyons went to the door and listened, his back to the corrugated steel of the warehouse. He heard a static-scratched voice shouting over a radio. The noise of the distant firefight blared behind some voices. Another voice issued orders from the quiet of a command post. Then he heard the exclamations of the men in the office. Lyons motioned Blancanales to the door.

The multilingual Puerto Rican listened. He held up two fingers—two men. Lyons pointed to himself and then inside. Blancanales nodded.

With his Colt held ready, Lyons eased open the door. He saw two men with their backs to him as they sat and listened to the radio exchanges of line officers and their commander. Lyons stepped up behind them and fired twice, one bullet for each man, the only sounds of the killing the slap of the bullets punching into their skulls and the actioning of the Colt's slide.

A chair scraped. Lyons turned to see three startled

soldiers rising from a desk where they had been studying a topographical map.

One soldier reached for a rifle leaning against a support post, and Lyons fired two quick shots into his back, spinning the dying man against the wall. Pivoting, pointing the Colt with both hands, Lyons aimed at the chest of another soldier and pulled the trigger.

Nothing. Brass stood in the slide of the Colt. A cartridge casing had failed to eject clear of the slide and the slide had closed on the casing, jamming the action.

The syndicate soldier clawed for the pistol in his flap-closed holster. Lyons rushed into him, throwing a full-power front kick into his solar plexus, and the soldier's breath exploded from his lungs. Lyons turned as the other soldier raised a long FN FAL fixed-stock rifle.

Simultaneously down-blocking with his left arm and grabbing the rifle's steel receiver, Lyons drove his left boot into the man's gut. Turning, Lyons pulled the rifle out of the falling soldier's hands and continued sideways with his weight, his boot coming down on the soldier's knee, breaking it backward as Lyons drove his boot down to the floor.

Lyons dropped the rifle. He turned the Colt over and snapped back the slide, ejecting the jammed casing to clear the action.

Slugs zipped past him, and the soldier on the floor took a burst of three low-velocity 9mm slugs in the face. A pistol fell from the dying man's hands. Blancanales fired a second burst into the third soldier's chest as he fell back. Lyons pointed the Colt autopistol straight down at the gasping soldier and fired once.

Gadgets closed the door and stepped over dead soldiers to the radio. After checking the setting of the frequency selector, he turned to his partners.

"I can do a number on their communications."

"Later," Lyons answered in a whisper. "We're looking for gasoline and explosives."

Gadgets nodded and turned off the radio. In the silence, Lyons went to the inside door. He motioned for Blancanales to kill the lights.

No light showed from inside the warehouse. They listened for a minute, then Lyons eased open the door. He crept a few steps to the side of the doorway and dropped to a crouch. He whispered to Gadgets, "Lights on."

A switch clicked and a worklight glared. Staying low, Lyons scanned the interior. Against one wall, construction materials—corrugated-steel sheets, steel beams, lumber, bags of cement—rose to the ceiling. Before another wall, drums of paint and solvent stood on pallets. A cement truck was parked in the center of the floor.

Wide, sliding doors led to the adjoining warehouses. Lyons motioned to Gadgets, and as Gadgets moved behind him, Lyons rushed to the nearest door. He listened, heard nothing on the other side.

Shoving the door open, Lyons switched on the lights and scanned the interior of the next building. Racks of plastic and iron pipe reaching to the ceiling. Bins of fittings lined the front wall.

Tons of fertilizers in plastic bags stood against

another wall. Insecticides and fertilizers—in drums, boxes, and bags—waited on pallets for shipment.

Lyons went back to Gadgets. "Nothing in there but farm equipment. Pipe, fertilizer."

Gadgets nodded. He went to the opposite wall and rolled aside the door leading to the other warehouse. Lyons waited as Gadgets slipped into the darkness, then he switched on the worklights.

"This is it!" Gadgets told him.

They saw a service area for trucks. Drums of solvents stood against one wall. A ten thousand liter steel tank with an electric pump stood against the other wall.

"Goddamn it!" Gadgets cursed. "Diesel fuel! Why don't they have something interesting, like avgas or nitromethane? Something that will make one totally righteous fire? Just that useless diesel.... Oh, yeah! The Wizard's got an idea! You said that other warehouse had fertilizer?"

"Yeah, tons of it. For their dope farms."

Gadgets ran to the warehouse of agriculture equipment.

"All right, ammonium nitrate!" Then Gadgets ran back to the racks of paints and solvents. Lyons saw the electronics specialist staring at the cement mixer. Gadgets turned to Lyons.

"If we can't make a fire, what about a big, big bang?"

16

"Guajiros are attacking the northeast plantation!" the radio operator shouted to Colonel Castro.

On the balcony, Colonel Castro passed the microphone of a field radio to one of his aides. "Maintain contact with all perimeter guards. We must be ready for an assault on another front from the western road or the mountains or the air." His arm swept across the panorama of flames as he indicated the vulnerable areas.

Then the colonel rushed into his office. He saw his son at the radio, questioning the distant officer and taking notes on the replies. He had spread out a map of the northeast facilities. Penciling in triangles, he indicated the direction and target of the Guajiro attack.

Proud of his son's prompt response to the alarm, the colonel did not take the microphone himself. He waited as Enrique completed his questioning and then he asked, "What is the information?"

"It is the same as last night. A cargo plane landed at the airstrip. They are now under siege. Because of the alert, they were ready. But the Guajiros have rockets and they are destroying the buildings one by one and killing everyone. It is very serious."

"So it appears that the attack here is only a diversion. . . . Is there any report of helicopters?"

"No. They came in a plane."

"Very good. Maintain contact with them."

"Will we send reinforcements?"

"Yes, but do not say that over the radio. The Guajiros might be monitoring our transmissions."

Enrique Castro snapped to attention and saluted his father. "I request permission to lead the reaction force."

"No, my son. You have responsibilities here," Colonel Castro said as he returned to the balcony.

Cursing under his breath, Enrique jerked his M-60 from the floor and tossed the belt of linked cartridges over his shoulder. As he left the office, Luis Ortega joined him.

"So you are still a boy."

"What?" Enrique spun around to face his friend. "What did you say?"

Ortega glanced up and down the corridor. No one in the colonel's office could hear him now. "It was like you have told me many times, was it not? You asked for an opportunity to prove yourself in battle and your father only laughed at you. I saw. Everyone saw. You are a man, you have courage, but to your father you are only a boy. And to him, you will always remain a boy."

Sneering, his acne-ravaged face twisting into a mask of hatred, Enrique looked back to the office. "Someday, someday I will take the business and the battalion from him!"

"Why not tonight?"

"What?"

"Why should the dying continue? The enemies of your father want only a share of the international trade. They do not want war, but they will fight until they win their rightful share. If you were to stop this fighting, to cooperate, you would be their friend. You could have the business, the battalion, all the property and the friendship of the other syndicates in Colombia."

"How do I do this?"

"Come with me," Luis Ortega said.

REVVING THE TRUCK'S ENGINE, Gadgets engaged the linkage driving the cement mixer. It turned. He switched off the engine and ran back to where Chandler and Davis stood with Lyons.

"You, Davis. You can work a skiploader?"

"Can do."

"Then I want you to bring over pallet-loads of that ammonium nitrate fertilizer from the other building."

"How much?"

Gadgets mentally totaled numbers. "Say...five tons. I think there's a half ton to the pallet. So we need ten pallets. Maybe we can put more in. And you, Chandler. There's a tank of diesel fuel in there, thousands and thousands of gallons. All we need. The tank's pump has got a hose on it. I need the hose to go in that cement mixer. It's not long enough, but there's all kinds of hose and pipe around here. Get it done."

"Sure, but what are you doing?"

"I told you, man. Making a bomb. Get to work, got no time to talk."

Across the warehouse, Blancanales snapped his fingers to get the attention of his partners. "Wizard!"

"On my way. Ironman. See those racks over there? I saw some drums of aluminum powder, for making aluminum paint. And some inflammable solvents. Get all the powder over here, then work on the solvents. Back in a flash.…."

Gadgets ran to the office, where Blancanales told him, "The Guajiros attacked some *finca* designated 'northeast.' Then an order came over the walkie-talkie to dispatch the helicopter unit. I went over to the hangar and confirmed it. All those soldiers waiting at the Hueys are on their way out."

"So the helicopter's a reaction force? What did they say on the long-range set about the helicopter unit?"

"Nothing. The order went out on the walkie-talkie."

Considering the information, Gadgets nodded. "Then they're thinking the Guajiros got one of their radios. No secure frequencies. No parallel frequencies. Am I going to do a number on them!" Gadgets opened up his electronics kit. "Keep watch on the doors, Pol. I'm going to be one busy dude."

"What are you doing?"

"Jamming, man!" He jerked open the back of the battalion radio. "It's all going to space noise. Walkie-talkies, radios, whatever. These gooners are going to be using pigeons to communicate."

Blancanales glanced at the cement mixer. "What role does the truck play in that?"

"You wait, you just wait." Gadgets looked up from the radio's circuits. "You know, it's times like this, when it all clicks, that I really fly. It's times like this that make it all worth it. I really feel like an artist, a real mover and shaker. And man, is this place going to shake."

LIEUTENANT LUIS ORTEGA maneuvered the staff car through the streets of the battalion base. Wreckage closed some streets. In others, groups of soldiers sprayed water on burning buildings, the fire equipment blocking the way and forcing Ortega to throw the car in reverse. He whipped the car backward through a turn, knocking down a wounded man. Accelerating away, Ortega gestured at the destruction and lectured Enrique Castro.

"This is what your father's mad ego creates. He will not compromise, he will not negotiate, he will not allow others to work for their rightful share—and this is what happens. The northern syndicates begged him to be fair. They begged him not to monopolize everything, but—"

Enrique interrupted Ortega's narration. "If I depose the old man, what will I get?"

"Everything that is his and all that his syndicate already earns. The only difference will be that the Guajiro syndicates have the right to sell their cocaine in North America and Europe. A right that your father has denied them."

"That is enough. Now how do I help you and how do you help me?"

Rotorthrob passed over the car. Lieutenant Ortega looked up and saw the silhouette of a troop helicopter against the stars. "Those are the best soldiers of the battalion, going to reinforce the northeast plantation, correct?"

"Right."

Sentries stepped in front of the car. One soldier shone a flashlight into Ortega's face and demanded, "What is your business here?"

Enrique Castro shouted at the sentries. "He is driving the car for me. That is his business. Now do you want to question me?"

The soldiers recognized the son of their commander. They saluted and backed away. "No, Lieutenant Castro. You are free to pass."

"Enrique, that is how you can help."

"What do you mean?"

Speeding away, they saw a second helicopter lift from the airstrip. Ortega parked beside a hangar where they had a view of the runway.

"All the men of the battalion know you. If you call out for a change in leadership, if you announce that you will lead the battalion and the syndicate into the twenty-first century, they will follow. Discontent is everywhere. The soldiers know that they fight and die only for the vanity of the old colonel. They will follow you."

Enrique shook his head. "But all the officers will stand with him. Without an equal force, they—"

"The force comes!" Ortega said as he took a field radio from the rear seat. "Minutes from now, the cadre of the new battalion will come. They need only your leadership to make the battalion and the syndicate obey your commands. Will you lead us into the future?"

"I want it all," Enrique declared.

Ortega flicked on the radio's power switch.

IN THE CORRUGATED-STEEL WAREHOUSE, the clanking and grinding of the cement mixer drowned out the noises of the fighting outside. Gadgets supervised the frantic loading of the mixer, directing the others with gestures.

Davis, Chandler and Lyons had formed a labor team. Using two forklifts to create a platform level with the mixer, they worked without pause. Davis operated a third forklift, raising pallet-loads of fifty-pound bags of fertilizer to the height of the platform. Chandler knifed open the waterproof plastic bags and passed them to Lyons, who emptied the sacks into the mixer.

Rope lashed the hose from the diesel tank in place, and the tank's pump shot a steady stream of the fuel into the mixer. As Gadgets ran from the truck-repair warehouse, he glanced at the pile of empty plastic sacks.

Climbing up the forklifts, he shouted over the noise to Chandler and Lyons, "Forget emptying the bags! Just cut them open and dump them in. Let the mixer empty them out."

Lyons did not pause in his work as he asked, "Won't that make a problem with the mixture of the—"

"What will make a problem is if we don't get it done! That plastic's flammable. It'll add to the effect."

Adjusting their routine, Lyons and Davis worked in tandem, both men slashing open the bags, then shoving the opened bags into the mixer. The change doubled their loading rate.

Gadgets climbed down to the floor, ran to the office and shut the door against the noise. Keying his hand radio, he whispered, "Pol, what goes on?"

The door eased open. Blancanales leaned in and reported, *"Nada."*

"Not now, that is," Gadgets said with a smile. "But the big surprise is on the way."

A RADIO OPERATOR rushed up to a group of officers conferring with Colonel Castro. The officers listened to the reports from the besieged plantation and made marks on a map. Finally the colonel looked up to see the radioman waiting.

"What is it?"

"I have the Guajiros."

"What? Where?"

"On the radio. They are transmitting in code, but—"

"Where is the radio?" The colonel turned to his officers. "Monitor the situation, and under no circumstances tell our men that the helicopters are already on their way."

The radio operator led the colonel from his office, across the corridor to the general's library. A field radio sat on the desk. Two clerks took notes on voices speaking brief sequences of code. The letters, numbers and phrases had no meaning to the clerks listening, but they continued transcribing the transmissions.

However, behind the voices speaking code the colonel heard a sound that instantly alerted him to a new threat.

Rotor noise.

The Guajiros were radioing from a helicopter in flight. As the transmissions alternated back and forth, the colonel listened closely. One voice radioed from a helicopter, the other voice radioed from an area of intermittent fighting. The colonel listened to a volley of rifle fire behind the voice.

Moving to the window, the colonel listened to the fighting in the village. He heard individual shots, a few autobursts, the bang of a grenade.

The same sounds came from the radio.

Did the radio transmit from the road, where the force of Guajiros fought to enter the village?

No. If the radio transmitted from one of the trucks, the battle noises would overwhelm the voice. Distance diminished the rifle reports and explosions. And the sounds seemed to come after an instant's delay.

The Guajiro radioed from the village or the base.

One of the townspeople? Possible. One of his soldiers? Impossible.

The colonel leaned over the shoulders of the clerks to read their notes. He recognized a pattern in the code. The numbers appeared to be casualty estimates, the numbers of his men already lost in the assault and the numbers of men still fighting.

Would someone in the village know those details?

The voice on the radio lapsed into uncoded speech. "It will be a success. I have secured the support of the man who will lead the syndicate after we put down the colonel. He will confirm this himself...."

There was a brief pause, and then a voice spoke crisply over the radio. "I am Enrique Raul Castro, son of the colonel. I welcome your aid and will join you in an alliance based on friendship and mutual opportunity."

Colonel Castro fell back, stunned by what he had heard.

His only son had betrayed him.

17

"Stop asking me what I'm doing!" Gadgets snapped at Chandler. "Ask Pol, he had the same training I did. He read the books."

Using his knife, Gadgets cut a slab of plastic explosive into equal cubes. Chandler left the electronics specialist and crossed the warehouse to the office. There, he saw Blancanales monitoring the battalion radio.

"The Wizard told me to ask you about what he's doing. Do you know?"

Blancanales nodded. "He's making the biggest improvised bomb I've ever seen or heard of."

"With diesel fuel and fertilizer?"

"And aluminum powder and a number of miscellaneous solvents. Our training manuals explained how to mix the components. There was nothing in the book about using a cement truck, but...why not?"

"Will it actually explode?"

"Maybe. The book says it will. We made a few improvised bombs in training and they made noise, but that was small-time. Correctly prepared, a diesel-ammonium-nitrate mix approaches fifty percent of the explosive power of TNT."

"Fifty percent?" Chandler turned and looked at the cement truck. "We put five tons of fertilizer in that mixer and pumped in all that diesel, so that's probably ten tons, total. You mean that the explosion might be the same as five tons of TNT?"

"If it explodes."

"Oh, wow...." Chandler considered the idea for a moment. "And where will we be?"

Blancanales laughed. "Far away, I hope."

Gadgets called out. "Pol! It's set. You ready to take your drive?"

"You're driving that bomb?" Chandler asked, incredulous.

"We don't want to blow away the airport, right? We want to create a panic so that the Castros will attempt to escape. So I'll drive the truck somewhere into the base." Again, Blancanales laughed. "Remember, until he pushes the button, it's only a truck."

As THEY LEFT THE STAFF CAR, Ortega detailed how Enrique Castro would deceive the soldiers guarding the airstrip. "The landing time will be the time of greatest risk. You must tell all the guards that the helicopters carry reinforcements from a friend of the colonel's. The men will be wearing army uniforms and carrying army weapons. The guards will not think they are Guajiros. Once they are out of the helicopters, our takeover begins. We will secure the airport area for the arrival planes carrying more soldiers."

"And if the battalion fights?" Enrique asked. "What if they do not desert my father?"

"After the Guajiro spread out, we will tell the soldiers that you are taking over the battalion. If they join us, good. If they fight, it will be too late. The Guajiros will eliminate the soldiers who will not follow you. Then we must hold the airport until the planes arrive."

"Is that possible? To hold the airport against all the battalion?"

"The battalion fights on the road. The battalion must fight the fires on the base. The battalion must guard against other attacks. How many men will the colonel have left to send into the fight? We can hold the airport. It can be done. We planned to do this without your leadership. We did not know you would join us. It will be the best Guajiro soldiers and the smart battalion soldiers who join us and the two helicopters against the demoralized battalion. It can be done."

As Lieutenant Ortega finished his speech, they approached the first machine gunner.

DRIVING THE CLANKING CEMENT MIXER from the row of warehouses, Blancanales wrenched the steering wheel through a right-hand turn and passed the vehicle yard. Ahead, he saw darkness and swirling smoke glowing orange with flames. The truck lurched and shuddered on the pitted asphalt road, the turning of the mixing bucket a continuing vibration shaking the entire truck.

Blancanales drove out through the same gate he had entered when he drove the stolen truck. As before, no soldiers stood guard, and he continued into the base. This time he did not have his partners behind him. Though Lyons had offered to accompany him, to literally ride shotgun, Blancanales had vetoed the idea. Blancanales would return to the airport on foot. Wearing the battalion uniform, speaking perfect Spanish, and with his dark hair and features, he had a good chance of slipping back to his partners unchallenged.

But could Lyons hope to pass for a Colombian army soldier or a syndicate militiaman?

So Blancanales went alone.

In the lowest gear, Blancanales eased the huge truck through the base. Soldiers hosing a fire stared as the cement truck passed, but they did not stop him. He came to a jeep blocking the narrow street.

The truck's airhorn got the attention of every soldier and officer within sight. A soldier called out to Blancanales in the elevated cab.

"What's your problem?"

"Get that jeep moved!" Blancanales shouted.

"Where are you going with that truck?"

"What's it to you?"

"Salute! You're speaking to a lieutenant!"

Blancanales saluted, then shouted again. "We're using this truck to block the road. It'll be impossible to move, even with rockets."

The officer believed him. Without another question, the lieutenant backed the jeep out of the way, and Blancanales continued to an assembly area. Barracks and offices lined the asphalt rectangle. Driving straight across, Blancanales guided the cement truck toward the palace overlooking the base.

Buildings were burning on both sides of the wide street he turned down, and ahead he saw a chain link and concertina wire gate blocking the approach to the colonel's mountaintop palace. He turned right before reaching the gate, the oversized tires of the truck crushing debris. Finally he pulled up in front of the smoking hulk of a truck. He could proceed no farther. Looking out the window of the cab, he saw the palace rising against the night.

Taking out his hand radio, Blancanales buzzed Gadgets. "I'm parking the truck. It's about fifty yards short of the white house."

"Okay, make it back quick! We got to get into motion, and we won't move until you're here."

"On my way," the Politician replied.

Taking his FN pararifle, Blancanales dropped to the asphalt and jogged through the base, looking like one of the many soldiers.

GATHERING HIS MOST TRUSTED OFFICERS together, Colonel Castro sketched the airstrip. He spoke in a slow, emotionless voice as he briefed them on the coming ambush.

"Guajiros will land in helicopters. I believe they will be the advance party for a main force. They will be aided by traitors on the ground—"

"Traitors! Who?" an officer interrupted.

His voice heavy with sorrow, the colonel avoided a direct answer. "It does not matter. We will deploy here, between the camp and the runway, with machine guns, rifles and rocket launchers. We will hold our fire until the helicopters touch down. As the

Guajiros disembark from the helicopters, I will fire the first shots. Is that understood? I will fire first. Questions?''

All the officers asked at once. "Who are the traitors?''

The colonel shook his head. "It does not matter. They will die. Go, gather your men.''

When the officers had filed out, the colonel spoke quietly to his aide. "I want the sniper rifle from the armory, the one with the Starlite device. Bring it to me.''

ENRIQUE CASTRO HAD SPOKEN with the soldiers guarding the airfield. Now, he and Lieutenant Ortega crossed the expanse of smooth asphalt to the trucks parked in the center of the runway to block the landing of planes.

"They believed you," Ortega said.

"Why shouldn't they?" Enrique asked.

Ortega offered Enrique a vial of cocaine. "It's vestiges of feudalism. Because you are the son of the leader, you are an important man.''

Snorting down half the vial, Enrique passed the vial back to Ortega. Ortega pretended to snort, then passed it back to Enrique, who finished the vial as Ortega talked.

"Now all the others will follow you. Feudalism demands loyalty on the part of the soldiers and daring on the part of the leader. Your decision tonight was very brave, and it comes at the most opportune time. You will see. Victory comes to he who dares, as the English say.''

"Yes! He who dares!" Enrique Castro raved, the cocaine already acting on his brain. "And no one is more daring than I."

At the trucks, Ortega leaned through a driver's-side window and saw that the keys were in the ignition. Behind him, Enrique Castro took a leather coin purse from the pocket of his fatigues. He pinched a gram of cocaine and snorted it.

Ortega wondered if the playboy would burn out his mind before the Guajiro assault on the battalion. But he did not stop the young Castro from taking more of the drug. Only with his mind totally twisted with cocaine would the playboy believe he could become the leader of the battalion. Only with his mind twisted could he believe he would be welcomed as an ally and equal to the Guajiro gang lords.

They walked two hundred feet to the next truck. Again, Ortega confirmed the keys. Though the Guajiro commando team could bypass the ignition locks, the wiring would take precious minutes, minutes that would delay the landing of the troop-carrying planes and the final assault on the Castro syndicate.

SOMETIMES RUNNING, sometimes slowing to a walk, Blancanales moved quickly through the disorder of the base. He paused at corners, peering ahead through the drifting smoke before starting down a street. He did not want to encounter a fire-fighting detail that needed soldiers. When troop trucks passed, he stepped back into the shadows. He had no time to talk his way out of a combat force.

Finally he came to the vehicle yard. He broke into a

sprint, making up for the time lost to caution. At the wide truck lane between the warehouses and the aircraft hangars, he slowed. He slowed his breathing, listening, watching. Nothing seemed different. The soldiers had not altered their positions. Only then did Blancanales continue to the door of the warehouse office.

"There he is," Lyons whispered from the shadows. "Ready to go?"

"Where are the others?" Blancanales inquired.

"Inside."

Blancanales heard his hand radio click as Lyons keyed the transmit button on his own radio. Gadgets looked out of the office.

"Any excitement?"

"Nothing. You got the radios wired?"

"Ready to zap. Here come the cherries...."

Struggling with the weight of tools and bundles of rope, Davis and Chandler staggered out. Blancanales went back to the truck they had driven into the area, and seconds later Lyons and Gadgets joined them.

"They are now listening to space noise," Gadgets told Blancanales.

Putting the truck in gear, Blancanales drove away from the warehouses. He followed the wide access lane past the aircraft hangars and continued to the far end of the runway. Turning, he crossed to the opposite side.

In the lighted interior of one hangar, he saw soldiers gathered around a radio. Another soldier spoke into a telephone. A hundred yards across the tarmac, a soldier held up a walkie-talkie and waved his arms to the others in the hangars. Blancanales did not need to hear their shouts to know Gadgets had succeeded in scrambling all radio communications. Only the telephones remained, and that meant no field units or patrols could receive instructions or relay information.

Blancanales continued to the midpoint of the runway. Across the wide expanse of asphalt, he had a clear view of the hangars. If the Castros attempted to flee in their planes, Able Team could choose the moment to make their kill. Only the two trucks blocking the runway interfered with their line of fire. And the Castros would order the trucks moved before they made their break.

Parking the truck next to the chain link and concertina wire perimeter fence, Blancanales got out. He went around to the opposite side, where none of the soldiers in the hangars could see him, and jerked out one of the stake panels.

"This is it," he announced to the others.

Staying low, Gadgets, Lyons, Chandler and Davis dropped out of the truck. Gadgets rushed over to the perimeter fence and tested it for electrical charge. "It's cold," he shouted back.

Lyons carried over the long-handled bolt cutters he had taken from the farm-supply warehouse. Working with Gadgets, he cut a flap in the chain link. Then Gadgets crawled through to the other side.

Flat on his belly, Gadgets examined the cleared ground around the perimeter for mines or sensors. He found none. Continuing out to the dropoff, he looked down the steep mountainside.

"Link up the ropes! This is almost a cliff."

Blancanales stood watch, and Lyons supervised Davis and Chandler as the two men passed the individual coils of rope through the hole in the fence, then carefully knotted the coils together. Lyons tied one end of the single huge coil of rope to a fence post, then signaled the two men to drag the rope out to Gadgets.

Grunting with the weight, spitting the white dust of the perimeter, they finally reached the edge.

"We're going down that?" Chandler gasped, looking down into the darkness.

"Unless you'd rather stick around," Gadgets joked. "After we blow the place away, then off the headman and the prince. I know they'd have some interesting payback for you."

Davis studied the drop. "No other way out of here? I like to do my flying in airplanes."

Distant, but unmistakable, they heard it.

Rotorthrob.

18

Only static came from the radios. Colonel Castro crouched beside the communications jeep as the operator tried to somehow correct the malfunction. The soldier spun through the shortwave frequencies on long-range radio, then tried the walkie-talkie. The radio operator shook his head.

"Colonel, it is only the battalion frequency. The other bands are clear. But the noise is also on the walkie-talkie. We cannot communicate with the other bases. And we cannot communicate with our units here."

"The Guajiros?" Colonel Castro asked.

"It must be," the radio operator replied.

"This has all been planned and coordinated," the colonel said to a lieutenant. "The attacks last night and tonight, the radios, the traitor...."

Then they heard the helicopters. The colonel stood and listened. "But the tricks do them no good! My soldiers, be ready!"

Rushing back to his position at the fence dividing the airstrip area from the base, the colonel picked up an FN FAL rifle. He took off the foam case protecting the Starlite scope and flipped the power switch.

All along the fence, soldiers readied their weapons.

Holes had been cut through the chain link for their rifles, machine guns and rocket launchers. Their weapons commanded the length of the runway. Only the parked trucks would provide cover for the Guajiros.

And the soldiers with the rockets had zeroed their launchers on the trucks.

Behind the line of men with direct-fire weapons, a mortar crew waited, the tube aimed, boxes of illumination flares and high-explosive shells ready. The first shell from the mortar tube would be a starshell to illuminate the airstrip in magnesium white light.

The Guajiros would have no shelter. And after the destruction of their helicopters, no retreat but death.

As the helicopters approached, Colonel Castro squinted through the eyepiece of the Starlite scope. The electronics created a pale green view of the trucks. He held the cross hairs on the truck. He breathed deeply to steady his grip and calm his mind. Shifting his aim, he swept the field-of-view across the runway. He found one of the soldiers near the hangars. The electronics did not define the face of the man.

The colonel thanked God for that small mercy. He would not see the face of his son when he killed him.

STEPPING OUT OF THE HANGAR, Lieutenant Ortega scanned the night sky. He turned and saw Enrique Castro snorting down another few grams of cocaine and noticed the soldiers and the technicians watching their commander's son snorting the powder. Enrique weaved unsteadily on his feet, his eyes fluttering as the drug rushed through his brain. The soldiers laughed.

Ortega ran to Enrique and, grabbing him by the arm, dragged him out of the light. Enrique tried to break Ortega's grip, flailing his arms, cocaine flying. Stumbling with drug intoxication, cursing incoherently, Enrique fell and rolled on the asphalt.

Controlling his rage, Ortega cajoled, "The helicopters are coming down. We must be there to welcome our friends. Come, we must go to welcome the many brave soldiers who have come to help you."

He put his arm around Enrique and helped him to his feet. Together they staggered to the center of the runway. Enrique raved, but rotorthrob drowned out his voice.

Looking up, they saw the descending helicopters.

Enrique lurched forward, waving his arms.

Ortega followed a step behind the drug-intoxicated playboy as the black helicopters descended. The lead troopship came down between the two trucks barricading the runway. The second Guajiro troopship came down a hundred yards behind the second truck.

As the skids touched the asphalt, soldiers in black uniforms jumped out. Enrique rushed to the Guajiros, his arms open in welcome.

Someone grabbed Ortega's sleeve. Looking back, he saw no one there. Rotor noise hid the crack of the rifle that came an instant later. As he continued on to the helicopters, the second bullet from the colonel's sniper rifle punched through his body.

LYONS WATCHED THE TWO MEN as they stumbled across the runway. He glanced up to the descending troopships. The helicopters showed no lights, and he saw only silhouettes against the stars.

Did these helicopters come to help the besieged garrison? To shuttle soldiers? Then why did they land so far from hangars? If they carried soldiers, why didn't they take the soldiers directly to the fighting on the road?

Had Gadgets's jamming of the radio frequencies alarmed the newcomers? Did they believe the attacking Guajiros had overrun the base?

No, an overflight would have revealed the continuing fighting.

These helicopters did not come as allies, Lyons decided.

Rushing to Davis, Lyons jerked the DEA pilot to his feet. "Flyboy, be ready to go! Something's going on and we're going to use it."

"What're you talking about?"

As the black troopships touched the runway, soldiers in black fatigues jumped from the side doors.

A flare burst, bathing the scene in white light, and high overhead a canister swung on a parachute. Suddenly, Chandler shouted out, "That's Enrique Castro! I see him there! With those soldiers!"

Lyons called out to Gadgets and Blancanales. "Kill that punk! And then we take that second helicopter."

Gadgets fired his Interdynamics-silenced Colt Assault Rifle into the chaos. Because the reduced-charge cartridges did not generate the force to cycle the action, he had to pull back the actuator to feed the next cartridge. In those two seconds he lost sight of Enrique Castro.

Rockets streaked across the runway. A black-clad Guajiro disappeared in an explosion as a warhead atomized his body. Another rocket missed the second helicopter, continuing past to explode in the distant perimeter fence.

Guajiro soldiers dropped as machine guns raked the runway. But the flashing muzzles of the ambushers gave away their positions. Rather than retreating to the troopships, machine-gun teams answered with lines of tracers.

Lyons grabbed Davis. "Follow me!" he shouted.

In his black fatigues, his blond hair and Anglo skin concealed by his *ninja*-style headcloth, Lyons sprinted diagonally across the few yards of open asphalt separating him from the second troopship.

Automatic-weapon fire rose to an overwhelming roar as he rushed the helicopter from the rear, the backs of the Guajiros to him. The intense noise hid the booms of his Konzak assault shotgun as he executed the few dope-syndicate soldiers on his side of the troopship.

From the truck, Gadgets watched in amazement. "What a dumb stunt! What would that crazyman do without me to back him up?" Gadgets flipped up the safety cover of his radio-pulse detonator and pressed the firing button.

A flash of red created an instant of daylight. Then came the blast, the explosion overwhelming the sounds of weapons and helicopters, the mountain shuddering as a vast fireball churned its way into the night.

The fireball's light showed the shaking hangars, the trucks swaying, the helicopters skitting about on their skids, the rolling of the runway's black surface.

All the shooting stopped. Stunned, the battalion defenders and the Guajiro attackers attempted to understand what impossible calamity had happened.

Lyons knew. He did not stop in his desperate rush. With his silenced Colt Government Model bucking in his hand, he killed a doorgunner, then jumped into the troopship. Looking across the tarmac, he saw Davis sprinting for the helicopter.

A Guajiro soldier looked back toward the helicopter. In the red light of the rising fireball, he saw a demonic figure, blue eyes glowing red. Then he died, a silent .45-caliber hollowpoint punching into his forehead.

Debris rained down, bits of rock and wood pinging in the spinning rotor blades. Objects fell everywhere as the blast-disintegrated base returned to earth.

Davis scrambled into the helicopter as Lyons leaned forward into the pilot's compartment. He saw only one pilot, the other seat empty. Lyons motioned Davis past.

Incredulous, but obeying, Davis squeezed into the empty copilot's seat. The Guajiro pilot looked away from the false sun in the night sky and saw Davis. Lyons put the end of the Colt's suppressor against the pilot's head.

But the pilot whipped around with a revolver. Lyons fired once, killing the Guajiro instantly, blood and gore spraying the interior as Davis struggled to maintain control of the troopship. Lyons ripped open the dead pilot's safety harness and pulled the corpse away from the controls. He dragged the corpse backward and threw it out the side door.

The Colt ready in his right hand, he grabbed his hand radio with the other. "We got the helicopter! We got it! Kill the Castro punk and we're on our way out!" Lyons shouted forward to Davis. "Get it moving! Over to the truck! Now! This is a killzone!"

Holstering his Colt, Lyons shoved the dead doorgunner out. He grabbed the pistol grip of the pedestal-mounted M-60 and turned the machine gun on the Guajiros.

As the helicopter lifted away, the Guajiro commandos turned. Lyons fired, raking the startled syndicate squad with point-blank 7.62 NATO rounds. He did not release the trigger as he swung the sights from soldier to soldier. Men flipped across the asphalt as tracers passed through bodies; the heavy-caliber slugs sent a rifle spinning through the air.

Davis held the helicopter in a low hover, the skids scraping the asphalt. The firing from the battalion had resumed. Now the Guajiros suffered in a cross fire, Lyons triggering bursts into every soldier he saw, the ambushers firing at both helicopters. Another rocket streaked out, and one of the trucks blocking the runway exploded.

Mortars fell, sending razors of shrapnel slashing through the exposed men. Lyons heard steel ping into the aluminum panels of the troopship. Raging with adrenaline, he screamed to his partners, "In! In! In!"

As they climbed through the side door, Lyons did

not stop to help them with their weapons and gear. He turned back to the M-60, aiming at the Guajiros crowding into the other helicopter, searching for Enrique Raul Castro as he sighted and fired burst after deadly burst.

The doorgunner in the first troopship returned the fire. Davis whipped the hijacked helicopter from side to side, then sideslipped behind the helicopter where the Guajiro doorgunner could not aim. But by rotating the troopship, Davis gave Lyons a direct line of fire.

Gadgets appeared beside Lyons with the M-16/M-203. The hybrid bucked, but the swaying of the hovering troopship threw off Gadgets's aim. The 40mm grenade passed under his target, exploding on the opposite side of the helicopter, killing and maiming the Guajiros rushing to climb aboard.

The pilot panicked. Lifting off with men hanging from the side door, the Guajiro pilot tried to escape. Davis took the hijacked helicopter after the Guajiros. Gadgets clawed out another 40mm shell and loaded the M-203.

Standing up behind the M-60, Lyons leaned out the side door, firing the machine gun straight down at the bodies. Lyons shouted back to Chandler. "You see him down there? The punk?"

"I think he made it into the helicopter!"

Lyons pulled grenades from his belt and threw the frags down into the tangle of dead and wounded. The grenades flashed as the helicopter left the runway behind.

For an instant they had a view of the battalion

base. A black smear, one hundred yards in diameter, ringed by fires, had appeared in the rows of streets and structures. The palace on the mountaintop had collapsed into white ruins.

"Wizard does it again!" Blancanales shouted.

Chandler only shook his head in amazement. He had heard narcs dream aloud of wiping out a dope gang, but these specialists actually did it.

Gadgets cut short the praise. Leaning into the pilot's compartment, he shouted over the noise of the rotors, "Get us close! I've got a grenade loaded."

"You can't dogfight in a helicopter!" Davis yelled.

"Who wants to fight? We came to kill!" Gadgets said.

"I'll do what I can...."

The hijacked helicopter, with the weight of only five men, gained on the other troopship. Davis stayed directly behind the other chopper's tail. The vast darkness of the jungle spread beneath them.

The four North Americans waited, ready for action, secured by safety straps. Lyons gripped the M-60, Gadgets the cocked-and-locked M-16/M-203. Blancanales and Chandler sat in the opposite doorway, Chandler with an M-16, Blancanales with a captured FN pararifle. Davis closed on the Guajiros.

The pilot attempted a maneuver, cutting his helicopter's airspeed, then simultaneously gaining altitude and rotating to give his doorgunner a line of fire at the pursuers. But the overloaded troopship responded too slowly. Davis veered away, then whipped a hard turn in front of and above the other helicopter.

For a second Lyons and Gadgets looked down on

the Guajiros. Lyons fired wild, his line of tracers crossing the tailboom. Gadgets aimed and squeezed.

The grenade scored an impossible hit, flying through the open side door to strike the side of the engine housing.

But he had loaded a white phosphorous shell. Gadgets shouted curses at himself as the searing white light glowed inside the Guajiro troopship.

Davis turned the helicopter through a figure eight and brought it back at the Guajiros, Blancanales and Chandler firing at the illuminated troopship. But before Davis could bring the helicopter around for another pass, the Guajiro pilot had gained speed again.

"Wizard screws up!" Lyons shouted.

"Yeah, yeah, I know. I should've checked the markings."

"Look!"

Leaning against their safety webbing, they saw the helicopter glowing white inside. A flaming man fell out, dropping into the darkness of the jungle.

"Hope it was the punk!" Lyons slipped on the doorgunner's headset. "Hey, Davis. Got any problems following that helicopter?"

"Quite a shot. Why didn't he just use high explosive and drop it out of the sky?" Davis asked.

"Just follow them."

"Won't be following them for long. That aircraft is due for a hard landing."

"When they go down, we want a confirmed kill on Enrique the punk. That means a body."

"Anything you say...."

Trailing smoke, the Guajiro helicopter managed to leave the vast Castro plantation behind. Davis followed the flames flickering from the fuselage as the helicopter weaved through the mountains.

But the Guajiro troopship finally lost power. The North Americans saw the helicopter autogyro into a mountainside. As they circled the flaming wreck, rifles flashed. Davis took the hijacked helicopter up out of range.

"The crash didn't kill them," Davis reported.

Lyons shouted to Chandler, "Castro might be dead, or he might be down there alive. I want to make sure."

After all he had risked, all the danger he had shared with these men, Chandler could not stop now. He shouted back, "I came to prosecute! Prosecute to the *max*!"

19

Dawn came quickly. The black night became blue, then a red fragment of brilliance appeared in the east, becoming a red disk. Within minutes, the white disk of the sun blazed down on the Colombian wilderness.

The hijacked Guajiro helicopter sat on a rocky ridge overlooking a horizon-spanning expanse of green. A few miles below, a line of smoke rose from the wreck of the Guajiro troopship.

After overflying the crash, Davis had found the ridgeline and landed by moonlight. The North Americans had spelled each other on sentry duty throughout the night. But only mosquitoes had attacked. No Guajiros attempted to take revenge.

In the first minutes of daylight, the five men started downhill through the dense jungle. They alternated on point, the first man using a machete from the helicopter's tool kit to hack through the vines and tangled undergrowth. The pointman hacked while the next man in line waited a few steps behind him, his rifle ready.

They labored for an hour, then found a much-traveled trail. Blancanales kicked a fly-buzzing heap of dung. Beetles swarmed out.

''Mule,'' he pronounced.

Lyons examined the trail for footprints. He walked a few steps in both directions, studying the trail's mud and matted leaves. "No boots. They haven't come this way. Do we want to risk this trail?"

Chandler answered first. "Sergeant Bolan told me to never take the easy way. Long time ago. And it kept me alive."

"You cut the way." Lyons gave the machete to the prosecutor.

Blancanales added, "This is a rush situation. If we want to confirm the death of Enrique Castro, we have to move quickly."

"And risk an ambush," Chandler countered.

"Great." Lyons laughed cynically. "Let's not keep them waiting."

Slipping the machete under his belt, Lyons jogged in the direction of the downed Guajiros. He did not look back to see if his partners followed. Gadgets laughed.

"There it is, the value of the Ironman. Think there's an ambush around the bend? Send him. He gets off on getting ambushed. He thinks it's fun to shoot in all directions. Demonstrate his superior firepower."

Then Gadgets followed. Blancanales turned to Davis and Chandler. "You can wait here," he said.

The two men looked around them. The overarching trees and vines reduced the morning light to semi-shadow. A few steps beyond the trail the jungle became impenetrable, a wall of green and shadow, concealing worlds of the unknown.

As Blancanales strode away, they followed.

Lyons moved quickly, but silently, a hundreds yards ahead. He advanced in starts and stops, walking fast, pausing for a moment to check a patch of mud for bootprints, then hurrying on again.

Other than the mule tracks, he saw only one other set of footprints. When he saw broken and torn fern fronds, he stopped. There, beside the marks made by the mule hooves, he saw the prints of small bare feet. Lyons studied the mud and oozing forest debris and tried to imagine the scene. The mule had stopped to eat the fern. A child riding the mule had slipped off the animal's back—Lyons saw where the small feet had landed in the trail. Then the child had broken off some fronds and remounted the mule. Totally innocent.

Lyons looked up from the marks on the earth to see an old man watching him. The old man stood in the center of the path, his white hair hanging to the shoulders of his white, patched and repatched peasant shirt. His frayed pants ended at the middle of his tanned, sturdy calves. The old man's features had the strangely Asiatic cast of an *indigena*.

The calm of the old man watching him unnerved Lyons. Lyons—the blond foreigner with an assault weapon slung on one shoulder, carrying grenades and a holstered autopistol, and an extended-patrol pack—did not frighten the old man. The old man carried no weapons. But he studied the blond foreigner with casual, and fearless, disdain.

Raising his right hand, palm open, Lyons simply said, *"Buenos dias, señor."* Then he reached across his web gear and gripped the sling of his Konzak. He pulled the sling forward to rotate the muzzle of the assault shotgun to straight down, away from the old man. The white-haired man watched as Lyons casually squatted, his arms resting on his knees, his empty hands dangling in front of him.

"What do you want?" the old man asked bluntly in his native tongue.

"Señor, I'm looking for a killer," Lyons answered, struggling with his bad Spanish. "A scum who killed a woman and a child."

"Who is this man? A Guajiro?"

They heard movement. The old man watched as Gadgets came up behind Lyons. "Greetings, señor. How are you?"

"We are waiting for the others," the old man told the two North Americans.

Lyons turned to his partner. "Make your weapons polite... very slowly," he said. "I think we are—"

"Being aimed at. Right, probably bows and arrows and maybe an RPG. And I thought you'd have it all wiped out by the time I made my appearance." Gadgets looked up at the unseen sky. "Beam me up, Scotty. This boy's in some very, very weird shit."

They waited until the others appeared. Blancanales tried to engage the old man in conversation, but the old man turned away. He said only, *"Seguame."*

Following him along the path, they heard others moving in the jungle. The men of Able Team watched the dense foliage, but they saw no one in the shadows.

"Thought the Ironman knew what he was doing," Chandler said to Gadgets. "We should have cut our own trail."

"You think this is a problem?" Gadgets asked.

"Damn right!"

"Look." Gadgets pointed to the trail. "Now that's a problem."

Chandler saw patterns of a rust-colored fluid splashed on the trail. Flies and insects fed on the splashes. In some places the fluid had puddled. And clotted.

Blood.

Gadgets watched Chandler's reaction, then said, "The Ironman's got a bad reputation for public relations, but we're walking to wherever. And we ain't bleeding."

"Yeah, I guess."

They heard voices ahead. Someone shouted in Spanish, the man's shout becoming pleading. Then the old man led the North Americans into a clearing.

The trail passed a village, and a high fence of thorn branches lashed together with hemp rope and vines blocked their view of the interior. Over the fence, they saw palm-thatched roofs.

A line of young *indigena* men emerged from the jungle. Like the old man, they wore peasant clothing. A few of the men sported bright soccer jerseys. One wore a long-sleeved black shirt, like the uniform worn by the Guajiro commandos. Others wore black nylon web gear, again like the belts worn by the Guajiros.

All the young men carried rifles. Some had old bolt-action rifles, while others carried FN paras. Though they held the rifles ready, no one pointed the weapons at the foreigners.

The group stopped at a gate in the fence. As the old man motioned for the foreigners to wait, children came to the gate and stared out. The men and teenagers with weapons stood along the fence, talking quietly with friends inside.

Using his backpack as protection against the thorns, Gadgets sat down against the fence. He took a pack of bubble gum out of his chest pocket and chewed a stick. The *indigenas* watched him. In the quiet, Gadgets could hear talk in the village.

Then came a sobbing moan of agony.

Davis and Chandler started, unnerved by the sound. Blancanales and Lyons watched the *indigena* riflemen. Gadgets snapped his gum.

The children stared as Gadgets blew a huge pink bubble, then he popped it and chewed the gum again. He looked at the children watching him. Taking the gum out of his pocket, he offered it to the children.

Two children ran away, but another boy and girl looked to the young men with rifles. A man nodded, and the children took the gum Gadgets offered. They put the pieces in their mouths without taking off the paper.

Gadgets shook his head and demonstrated how to unwrap the gum. The children followed his directions. As they chewed, they discovered the bright colors on the inner wrapper and squealed. They ran away laughing and chewing and waving the bright bits of paper. The men guarding the foreigners laughed.

Lyons laughed. "Prepare for an assault by hundreds of bubble gummers," he said.

"Yeah, maybe I did the wrong thing. . ." Gadgets wondered aloud.

"No, you didn't," Blancanales added.

Glancing to the young men with the rifles, Gadgets grinned. He unslung his CAR and leaned it against the thorns. Then he shrugged off his pack and unzipped the side. He pulled out a plastic box. Inside, he had more bubble gum.

Chandler looked at the gear and boxes inside Gadgets's pack. "Maybe you shouldn't let these people see all those good things you have in there. They might jump us just for—"

"This isn't San Diego, Counselor," Lyons interrupted. "I've never encountered an *indigena* who steals. That is, outside of a tourist resort."

The old man returned and talked with Blancanales. The others waited as Blancanales questioned and listened to the long answers. The old man gestured toward the mountain, then pointed inside. Blancanales gave the others a summary.

"They've got Castro, but they won't give him to us. Some children out gathering fruit found the helicopter early this morning. As they approached the wreck, Enrique shot one of the children. The rest of them went for help and these men fought it out with the Guajiros and killed them. They captured Enrique and another man, who bled to death. They won't give up Enrique because he murdered the child and they think he's some kind of demon from space, apparently because of the way he cut up the child with a machete."

Chandler nodded. "Like the lifeguard. That Castro punk is insane. A psychopath. These people are going to kill him? Are they sure it's Enrique Castro?''

Turning to the old man, Blancanales asked questions. The old man answered and pointed into the village. "They won't kill him, he said. But he will die. If we want, we can make the identification, but we absolutely must not interfere, the old man says. He says he'll let us see the criminal because he also did our people wrong.''

"We're supposed to go in there?'' Chandler asked, looking into the village. "Dangerous,'' he said, shaking his head.

Lyons laughed. "They didn't need to bring us here to trick us. Let's go take a look at the prisoner.''

As the group entered, children crowded around Gadgets. He walked along breaking pieces of gum in halves, so that twice as many children got the exotic treat to taste. The group of foreigners passed many empty huts.

Then they saw the shoulder-to-shoulder crowd in the center of the village. Men and women stared at the foreigners. Adults shooed the laughing children away. Only adults could attend this gathering.

"Buenos dias, buenos dias," the foreigners said to everyone. Some of the *indigenas* returned the greeting in Spanish, others turned away.

"So where is he?'' Chandler asked.

The crowd parted for the foreigners. What they saw stopped them in midstep. Chandler groaned and looked away. Davis stared and coughed as he choked down vomit.

Able Team had seen it all—they thought. Gadgets studied the scene with the detachment of a technician, then exclaimed, "Far, far out!" He set down his pack and found a camera in one of the pockets. As he snapped photos, he asked, "Is that him, Prosecutor?"

"That's him," Chandler answered, choosing not to look again.

"Can't think of it happening to a nicer guy," Lyons said with a smile.

Blancanales studied the horror and then spoke with the old man. As the old man narrated, Blancanales translated for the others.

"They took hammers to his hands so that he would never kill again. And so that his ghost would never walk back to their village, they hammered that stake through his legs...."

Fire-hardened and sharpened to a needle point, a hardwood stick an inch in diameter passed through Enrique Raul Castro's thighs, through the right and then on through the left. The stick had been secured in place with lashings of rope.

"And they cut the tendons of his legs...and then they fixed his arms," the Politician continued.

A second hardwood stick passed through Castro's arms, entering above the right elbow, passing through the right arm, then behind his back. The stick then passed through his left arm. Again, ropes bound the stick in place and other ropes bound the stick to an upright pole. The pole held Castro in a kneeling position.

"They cut off his genitals because a man would not kill a child...."

Blood puddled under the naked man's crotch.

"They cut out his tongue because he screamed blasphemies, and then they gouged out one eye and stuck it on a stick so that he could watch himself die."

Gadgets got a close-up of the impaled eyeball. Then he snapped a picture of the dying man's face. "What a strange point of view. You think he's actually seeing himself? If he squinted down real hard, do you think he could see his own reflection in his own eye? This is flat-out metaphysical."

"What do you think, Prosecutor?" Lyons asked. "You want to leave this case to the locals? Or maybe you want to force them to extradite him to San Diego? Personally, I'd say justice is done."

Chandler nodded. Forcing himself to look at the dying man, he finally said, "Justice is done. Wizard, get a good picture for me. Because my friends in the D.A.'s office will want to see this."

Squatting a few steps in front of Castro, Gadgets aimed his camera and whistled. "Hey, smile for the camera, tough guy. Used to be a bad man. No more. Now you're just fly food on a stick."

Enrique Raul Castro heard the English and looked up with his one eye.

A white flash blinded him. As he relapsed into semiconsciousness, he heard someone pronounce, "Case is closed. Prosecuted to the *max*!"

MORE GREAT ACTION COMING SOON

ABLE TEAM

#18 Tech War

Intercept or Destroy!

A U.S. argon ion laser that can etch the entire NORAD defense computer on a chip has been stolen and is on its way to Russia.

It's a high-tech threat capable of neutralizing U.S. defense capacity, and the President authorizes Able Team to take "any action necessary" to block the transshipment. It's a computer endgame and a new war—a Tech War.

Mack Bolan's

ABLE TEAM

by Dick Stivers

Action writhes in the reader's own street as Able Team's Carl "Mr. Ironman" Lyons, Pol Blancanales and Gadgets Schwarz make triple trouble in blazing war. To these superspecialists, justice is as sharp as a knife. Join the guys who began it all—Dick Stivers's Able Team!

"This guy has a fertile mind and a great eye for detail. Dick Stivers is brilliant!"

—*Don Pendleton*

Able Team titles are available wherever paperbacks are sold.

GOLD EAGLE

**Nile Barrabas and the
Soldiers of Barrabas are the**

SOBs

by Jack Hild

Nile Barrabas is a nervy son of a bitch who was the last
American soldier out of Vietnam and the first man into a
new kind of action. His warriors, called the Soldiers of
Barrabas, have one very simple ambition: to do what the
Marines can't or won't do. Join the Barrabas blitz! Each
book hits new heights—this is brawling at its best!

GOLD
EAGLE

Available wherever paperbacks are sold.

An epic novel of exotic rituals
and the lure of the Upper Amazon

THE TAKERS RIVER OF GOLD

Journey to a lost world on the edge of time…

Deep in the steaming heart of the Brazilian rain
forest there lurks a forgotten world, a fabled world—
the lost city of the Amazon warrior-women. But as
adventurers Josh Culhane and Mary Mulrooney
probe deeper, the uncharted jungle yields an even
darker secret—a serpentine plot so sinister it
challenges the farthest reaches of the mind.

Best-selling novelist Jerry Ahern, author of
The Survivalist and *Track*, once again teams up with
S. A. Ahern to boldly combine myth and fiction in a
gripping tale of adventure in the classic tradition of
Journey to the Center of the Earth and
Raiders of the Lost Ark.

Culhane and Mulrooney are The Takers.
You've never read adventure like this before.